MW00930178

Thank You and Bonus Novel!

I'd like to take a moment to thank you for your ongoing support. You make this all possible! To really show you my appreciation for purchasing this book, I'd love to send you a full-length horror novel in 3 formats (MOBI, EPUB and PDF) absolutely free!

Download your full-length horror novel, get free short stories, and receive future discounts by visiting www.ScareStreet.com/DavidLonghorn

See you in the shadows,
David Longhorn

PROLOGUE

Declan Mooney had been trying to tune his portable radio to the BBC's sports channel for roughly fifteen ever-more frustrating minutes. He eventually resorted to hitting the radio, fairly gently, then gave up rather than risk smashing it. He decided to check the scores on his phone instead but got just one bar and no useful service.

"Bugger," he told the empty office.

He told himself this was just a nuisance, that the huge aluminum box he was charged with guarding was the problem. It stood to reason, after all, that the sheer amount of metal in the vast storage facility would interfere with reception. And the way the lights flickered, and the fact that his walkie talkie reception was poor to lousy—they, too, could be blamed on the fabric of the building.

It's nothing like Rookwood, he told himself for the hundredth time.

If Declan had had a choice, he would not have opted for a night watchman's job in a place like this. It was a labyrinth of corridors lined with locked doors. He would have preferred a day job with plenty of people around, but beggars couldn't be choosers. And besides, nothing unusual had actually happened.

And yet... I can't bear to sit here in silence.

"I need me some noise," he said, and found a playlist on his phone. It was noisy, abrasive rock music, without too much thought behind it. Instant coffee for the brain, it made ideal listening for a long, lonely night in a big, gray box. But even the raucous tones of mediocre guitar bands fronted by forgettable white guys who couldn't really hold a note seemed to fail Declan tonight.

The problem was, during the odd quiet moment, and during the brief pauses between tracks, Declan felt sure he heard something.

Sensed something, anyway. He kept flicking through the feeds from various security cameras on the screens in front of him, hoping to see some dumb kids who had broken in, perhaps to have it off out of the rain, or take whatever street drug was in fashion. But every sweep showed nothing but empty corridors and closed roller-doors, like a never-ending series of garages for undersized cars.

When he had started this job, he had tried to imagine what was actually in each of the lock-up units. He had begun by imagining the proceeds of crime, untold riches in jewels, bullion, stolen artworks. Then he decided that international master criminals probably wouldn't stash their ill-gotten gains in Tynecastle.

Then he had tried to imagine stuff that compulsive hoarders might stash away because they couldn't bear to part with it. That, unfortunately, left him with too many options, from authentic Klingon costumes to bellybutton lint. He decided people might be storing perfectly sensible things they couldn't put anywhere else, which was boring, but certainly true in most cases.

"What the...?"

Declan killed the music in the middle of a long, derivative guitar solo. Something had snapped him out of his reverie; a noise that was loud enough to be heard above the music. Had he been wearing headphones—something he'd been specifically warned against—he would never have heard it.

The sound came again. It was muffled, distant, but had a metallic boom about it. Something had either struck the wall of the structure or one of the lock-up doors. He flicked through the camera feeds again but saw no sign of movement. The noise came a third time, a dull tinny thud. Declan jumped up, grabbing his walkie and his flashlight. He had no weapon, but he had a duty to investigate.

"Terry," he hissed into the handset. "Terry, can you hear me?"

Terry was the guard on the other unit, which was only a few yards away. But the hiss and crackle that came over the walkie meant they might as well have been on different planets. Declan picked up the internal phone but got no tone. It was dead.

"Crap."

Declan fought an impulse to simply ignore the noise, knowing he would lose his job if he screwed up. He could not afford to be fired. He left his office, trying the walkie at regular intervals, but continually getting nothing. The lights were flickering again, and his torch seemed inclined to join in. He tapped the flashlight, restoring full beam, and walked on. The erratic sounds were now almost continuous, a kind of rumble that suggested a malfunctioning washing machine. As he rounded a corner, he felt the temperature plummet, and wondered if an outer door was open.

No, the alarm would have gone off.

The metallic thumping was coming from this row of lockups. Declan raised his torch and flicked it up and down the corridor. The churning noise rose and fell, and was punctuated by a startling bang. He saw one of the roll-up doors bulge outward. Now, he knew what was happening. Nobody had broken in. Somebody was trying to get out. Declan heaved a sigh of relief.

Some idiot locked themselves in. God, maybe somebody decided to spend the night rather than go home, then thought better of it.

Declan stopped outside the unit, examined the check-in sheet hanging by the door. In theory, everyone accessing their lock-up should sign in and out. But according to the sheet, nobody had been in for over a week. He shrugged. People often ignored the rules. He moved closer to the corrugated metal door, listened to the odd bumps and thuds from inside. It still sounded vaguely mechanical, but not entirely. It was almost as if some kind of miniature tornado was swirling around inside, occasionally hurling small but fairly solid objects against the walls and door.

"Hello again, Declan."

He almost fell, turning around quickly just as the lights failed completely. His flashlight picked out a large, unmoving figure back along the corridor. The churning noise grew. There was another sound underneath it. Something was being ripped or torn apart. Paper.

"Who is it?" Declan demanded.

The flashlight beam revealed very familiar garb, camouflage trousers above heavy boots, a dark jacket, and a face concealed by a ski mask. In the intruder's right hand was a long gun. It was an Armalite. The American rifle was the weapon of choice for the kind of men who had long ago, in a city across the Irish Sea, sworn to kill a young 'traitor' called Declan Mooney.

"You're not real!" he shouted, stumbling away from the apparition. "You weren't real in Rookwood, you're not real now."

"Oh, Declan, we've all come a long way since Rookwood."

The gun came up as Declan froze, fear vying with reason. A shot rang out, deafening in the confined space. The left side of his body erupted with pain, the agony blossoming under his ribcage. He slumped against the metal wall, dropped his walkie, and clutched at his jacket, expecting to feel blood pumping through his gloved fingers. But there was nothing.

It was all a trick, he thought. *All an illusion. Just like before.*

And then he died.

***

November in Tynecastle, he thought. *It's bloody bleak.*

Detective Sergeant Nathaniel Farson was on his way to check in for the night shift. The weather was wet and cold, a steady drizzle soaking anyone unwise enough to walk outside sans umbrella. Farson, snug in his police Ford, was at least spared that. Or so he thought. But, as soon he took the turn off toward the old Tyne Bridge, he realized he was going to have to get out and get wet, after all.

Flashing lights ahead and a queue of traffic meant a problem on the bridge. Farson toyed with simply sitting in the queue, calling in to the control room to say he was stuck. He was heartily sick of police work in all its forms. But then he reasoned that, if he intervened, he would at least get a few brownie points. It did not pay to piss off the top brass too much, and Farson had made a nuisance of himself lately.

The detective got out and immediately stepped into a rain-filled pothole. Cursing, he dodged between stationary vehicles and got to the police cordon, where a fresh-faced young constable was arguing, in a desultory way, with a group of irate drivers.

"I don't care if she does chuck herself in the river," one man was saying. "I've got a delivery to make, and I'm already late!"

"And your work ethic does you credit, sir," said Farson drily, as he slipped under the barrier. At the same time, with practiced ease, he showed the youngster his ID.

Farson quickly established that a girl of about twenty was clinging to the rail of the bridge from the outside. The young constable had tried to talk to her, but she had not seemed to hear him. Now, a priest was 'having a go', as the uniform put it. A trained negotiator was on the way.

"I don't suppose he'll mind if I have a go, too," Farson remarked, walking into the shadow of the vast, cast-iron arches. The bridge, built in the mid-nineteenth century, had long been a magnet for potential suicides. Farson had talked one down himself, in his days as a regular patrolman.

He could make out the priest, a white-haired man in a raincoat. The girl was crouching on a narrow ledge and holding onto the metal mesh behind her. She wore jeans and a black hoodie. Her dark hair was plastered down over her face. The detective wondered what the priest might be saying, and hoped it was not too religious. In his experience, the young did not respond well to piety.

"Excuse me, sir, how are things going?" he asked quietly.

The white-haired man looked around, and Farson could see from the priest's expression that he did not think things were going very well. He gently suggested he take over for a while and moved along the inner edge of the rail until he was almost within grabbing distance of the girl. For a moment, he thought he might actually be able to haul her to safety. She seemed oblivious to Farson.

"No," she said suddenly, and shuffled sideways a few inches. "No, don't try it."

Farson stopped, held up his hands in a placatory gesture, but she did not look up. He wished he could see her face, gauge just how far she had gone down the road of despair. He glanced down, and felt his heart miss a beat. He was not looking at the rain-spattered surface of the River Tyne. He was looking at a car park fifty feet below, where another couple of uniforms were trying to hold back gawkers.

Oh, Christ, this could be a bad one.

As he looked up at the girl, she turned her head and for the first time, he saw her eyes. They were light gray in the poor light, might perhaps be blue by daylight. She looked coolly at Farson, not appearing to be agitated.

"Hi," he said. "I'm Nathaniel. I'm a police detective. I just happened to be passing, believe it or not. What's your name?"

The girl seemed to consider the question, then smiled and shook her head. At the same time, Farson caught sight of the vicar in his peripheral vision and turned to wave the man back. But there was nobody near him. Annoyed with himself, he switched his attention back to the girl. She was still smiling, and nodded as if he had confirmed something for her.

"You can see them, too!" said the young woman. "You can, can't you? You've seen them before, maybe."

"Maybe," Farson said, trying to shake off the odd sensation of someone standing near him. "But forget—forget them, let's talk about you. Won't you tell me your name?"

She shook her head.

"My name is not important, officer. I won't be needing it much longer."

Oh God, he thought. *This is not a cry for help.*

"Here they come," she said, sounding more excited. "All here for me. They told me to come here. They made it all really clear. I was wasting my time with the pills, talking to people, silly little mantras about how strong I am. Nobody gets out of this alive."

The girl braced herself, clearly preparing to jump.

"Don't!" Farson exclaimed and lunged for her. He managed to catch hold of her black hoodie. Again, he had the sense they were not alone, and this time he felt a piercing chill as dark figures moved on the fringe of vision.

"Don't feel bad about it, Nathaniel," said the girl, and wriggled out of her hoodie. She fell forward, for all the world as if she were plunging into a swimming pool. There were screams from below as Farson closed his eyes. A loud metallic crash, the breaking of glass, the irate tone of a triggered car alarm. It was over.

Farson looked down and saw colleagues clustered around the girl's motionless body. An ambulance had been standing by, but he doubted if its team could do any good. He began to walk back toward his car, still clutching the hoodie. The intense cold he had felt a few moments earlier had vanished, replaced by the familiar chill of a damp November evening.

"Sorry," he told the young constable. "I'll deal with the paperwork, make it clear you couldn't have stopped me."

The officer said something hard to make out over the sound of car horns blaring. Some drivers clearly felt that, now the girl was gone, there was no good reason to obstruct honest citizens.

"Sorry, what was that?" he asked.

"Who were those other guys?" the constable asked, eyes wide. "I mean, was there anybody else there?"

The priest appeared, put a hand on the officer's arm.

"Best not to ask about that, lad," the old man said. "Some things are better left alone. My faith tells me such things are sent to delude and ensnare us."

Farson hesitated, wondering how much more the priest might know. Then he decided he had enough on his plate. Spooky Farson, as he was known in the canteen, did not need to probe any more mysteries. He took charge of reopening the bridge, then continued his journey to work.

When he arrived, he found he was assigned what the duty sergeant called 'another bloody weird one'.

***

"Two in one night," Farson murmured as he stepped aside.

Two paramedics were wheeling a body out on a gurney. The detective stopped them for a moment and lifted the blanket covering the dead man's face. He glanced at it, then did a double take. The bald, bearded man looked familiar. He let the blanket drop and waved the paramedics on, thanking them absentmindedly.

"Okay," he said to the officer waiting inside the doorway, "fascinate me further."

The constable led him to a lock-up with a badly battered door. It looked as if it had been kicked or otherwise buffeted from the inside.

"They found the night watchman there," she said, gesturing. "He sent some kind of garbled message to a colleague in the next building. Guy found him dead and called us, so—"

"Rooney?" Farson said. "Or was it Mooney?"

The young woman looked surprised.

"Yeah, his name was Declan Mooney—was he a villain?"

Farson shook his head, ran his hand down the dented door.

"No, just a witness in a case. Poor bastard seems to have come down in the world. What's in here?"

After a short while, they found some bolt cutters and removed the padlock on the door. Farson half-expected to find more bodies, but instead, he saw a tiny, windowless room full of confetti. He clicked on the light and went inside, examined the shredded paper—the remnants of books, dozens of them. Under the chaos, he noticed cardboard boxes that had been thrown around as if by a whirlwind.

Or a maniac.

"Do you think the night watchman did this, sir?" asked the

8

constable.

"Why?" asked Farson. "I'm intrigued—do you think our minimum wage employee removed the padlock, tore up all the books, shut the door, and relocked it, then dropped dead? I don't know what your idea of a fun evening is, constable..."

There was a long silence as he continued to investigate. He found a ripped but otherwise intact leaflet, turned it over. The title was BEYNON BOOKS, with a snail mail address and a phone number. There was also, he was pleased to see, an email address. Inside the leaflet promised *Rare Books, Antiquarian Books, Unusual Books, Enjoyable Books...*

"Bloody expensive books," the detective murmured, bagging the leaflet.

"Evidence, sir?" asked the constable.

"I'm going to go out on a limb," Farson said. "And hazard a guess that this lock-up belongs to an antiquarian book dealer."

The young officer kicked a large heap of brownish paper debris.

"Reckon he's going to be a bit short of stock, then."

CHAPTER 1

Hell was a labyrinth of magic mirrors.

Everywhere she turned showed a fresh image, all different, yet all reflections of the same soul. Annie Elizabeth Semple was revealed again and again, in all her vileness. Every mirror showed a story set in a different world, each one centered on versions of the tormented soul who called herself Liz. Here she was a vile, plague-bearer, twisted body covered with sores, pus oozing through her foul rags. Then she saw a monstrous creature, hairy and bestial, fangs and claws clotted with gore. More often than any other of her many selves, she saw an excrement-smeared lunatic, chained up in a padded cell.

Even worse were the subtle, attractive images that gradually revealed the disgusting reality underneath. Liz saw herself as a fine lady, a busy young mother, even a heroic nurse in wartime. But every seductive reflection changed subtly in a moment, revealing the evil glint in the eyes, the deranged expression distorting the face. The fine lady poisoned her husband, the young mother smothered her offspring, the nurse left wounded heroes to die. Every possible variant of Liz that her imagination could conceive was evil.

"But they are not you, Liz. None of them are you!"

Paul Mahan struggled to get through to the tortured creature who cowered in the shining maze. He urged her to smash the mirrors, as he had done many times before. In earlier shared nightmares, Liz had not dared to try and break free. But recently, she had exhibited more bravery. Paul had cause to hope that the courage she had shown before might reemerge and liberate her from this torment.

"I can't do it," she wailed. "I am a monster, I'm evil, I've done terrible things!"

"You can, just smash the goddamn glass!" Paul insisted. "You've got the power, Liz, you know you have—now use it!"

Liz remained curled in a ball amid the ever shifting, ever shining mirrors of her soul. Paul, frustrated, reached out to try and touch her. He had never attempted that before, but his dream-hand did connect with the girl's bare shoulder. She flinched, looked up from under an untidy mop of dark hair.

"You can kill people with your mind," Paul said, brutally. "So why can't you break a few sheets of glass?"

Too late, he realized he had crossed a line, probed too deeply into the source of all her self-loathing. Liz's expression changed, her face becoming mask-like, her eyes devoid of feeling. Her eyes seemed to grow until they merged, became a single, lightless void. The last trace of radiance vanished, and he was in his own personal hell, a place of utter loneliness, with all hope of human contact gone. Paul flailed against nothingness, tried to scream in airless, starless space.

Suddenly, light returned, albeit a dim, unearthly radiance. Paul knew at once he was Liz, the newly dead girl haunting the half-burned East Wing of Rookwood. He had been drawn into her mind, and now she was reliving some crucial event. He guessed it must be the wrong she had once done, the 'crime' that led her to condemn herself.

"No, no, Liz!" he protested. "Let me go! Let yourself go free, don't relive this."

Instead, their point of view shifted, and Paul seemed to float along empty, smoke-blackened corridors until he reached a broken window. Outside, it was night. The grounds of the asylum seemed deserted. But then there was movement, a diminutive figure in short pants, sneaking timidly toward Rookwood. As the boy got closer, Paul saw he was about twelve and dressed in antiquated clothing, the sort of slightly comical outfit English boys wore in the years after World War Two. The boy glanced back a couple of times. It seemed someone was watching from the edge of the grounds.

As soon as the boy clambered through the window, Liz whispered to him, entering his mind. His name was Micky. He was shy and self-conscious about his size, desperate to fit in, be one of Tommo's gang. Liz saw Tommo in his mind, the swaggering bully who had forced the boy to go into the haunted building as a test.

Liz felt her rage return, and Paul once more experienced the cold fury that had allowed the girl to kill Palmer at the very climax of his last experiment. She was angry on behalf of the lonely little boy this time, wishing she could set things right for him, for all the victims who suffered and had no one to help them. Liz spoke to the boy, mind to mind.

'He's lying to you, Micky. Tommo will never let you in the gang, he's just trying to make you look stupid. He wants you to pee yourself and run away, screaming like a little girl. You don't need his gang, Micky. You can be brave and rely on yourself, make real friends. Just find the courage inside you. Tell Tommo and his gang to piss off...'

The boy smiled, straightened up, no longer cowering in the dark. He turned to clamber back out of the East Wing and froze. Suddenly, Paul sensed another presence, one that was all too familiar. Palmer was suddenly locked in conflict with Liz, battling to try and control the boy. The purely mental struggle was still intensely vicious, with Palmer marshaling his retinue of weaker victims against Liz. But still, Paul felt, the girl was strong enough to defy the amoral doctor.

And then Liz gave up.

Paul felt her retreat from the psychic fray, then saw Micky slump against the wall as Palmer took possession of his young, vulnerable mind. Liz withdrew from the East Wing, heading into the heart of the building. Paul knew what would happen next; that Palmer would bring the worst impulses of the boy to the surface. A death would result; Tommo the bully stabbed with a shard of broken glass. The press reports from the time called it a senseless killing.

"Why did you stop fighting, Liz?" he demanded. "That's not like you. I saw what you did to Jeff Bowman when he threated Ella and Neve."

The answer appeared in his mind. Micky had appeared just a few months after the disaster at Rookwood. At the time, Liz did not know whether Palmer could overwhelm her. She dreaded being defeated and enslaved in death after she had triumphed over him in life. Unsure of her strength, she had chosen to flee. With the benefit of hindsight, she could have won the battle for the boy's soul.

"You can't blame yourself for that," he insisted, as he found himself back in the hell of mirrors. "Liz, forgive yourself for that moment of weakness!"

She looked at him blankly, shook her head. A burst of energy struck him, sent him hurtling far above the bizarre glass maze. The labyrinth where Liz lay trapped by her own guilt shrank to a tiny point of light. All around him was darkness, an eternal void.

"Nooooooo!"

Suddenly, the darkness parted, as if a curtain had been drawn back. A vast, curved surface appeared, and Paul wondered if it was the surface of some strange planet. Then the murk cleared enough for him to see it was a face, or part of one. Paul saw very fine, golden hairs on the skin. He turned his head and saw enormous lips moving, forming syllables.

"… Three. Two. One."

The woman's calm voice raised him from his reverie. He gazed up at the anxious features of Doctor Blume. After he recognized her, he realized she was leaning over him as he lay on her therapy couch. Behind her stood Mike Bryson, looking down anxiously.

"Thought we'd lost you there, mate," said Mike. "She kick you out again?"

Paul glanced around the office, remembered where he was and what they were doing. Or trying to do.

"Yeah," he said grimly. "I couldn't get her to break free, but she felt confident enough to give me a smack in the kisser, or it's psychic equivalent. Something like that, anyhow."

"Was Ella there this time?" Mike asked.

"No," Paul said, smiling. "No, she's been absent for the last few sessions. Thank God. So that worked."

"I must recommend we cut back on these experiments," said the doctor, as she and Mike helped Paul up. "Here, drink some water—I know you are anxious to help Ella, but taking on her entire burden might not be the best way."

Paul wobbled, spilled some of the plastic cupful of water, and plopped down on the couch again. He ran quavering fingers through his hair and wondered if it was going gray yet.

"If you can think of another way to take the heat off Ella," he said, not meeting Blume's eye, "I'd like to hear it. She and I are the only people with this tie to Liz, the only people she can reach out to, cling to."

"Yeah," said Mike quietly, sitting down next to Paul. "But, look at it this way—if you have a breakdown, or whatever, you can't help Ella, or Liz. You'll just wreck your own health."

Paul nodded, unable to refute his friend's commonsense. Since he had started these off-the-record sessions with Blume, he had endured tremendous stress. Blume's use of suggestion to put Paul into Liz's personal hell had been Paul's idea, attempted against the therapist's advice. But since Blume had been confronted with clear evidence of the paranormal, she had been willing to help. This was, Paul suspected, partly from guilt at having at first dismissed his experiences at Rookwood as symptoms of mental illness.

"Let's check with Neve," Mike said finally, taking out his phone.

Ella's mother confirmed her daughter was sleeping peacefully. Mike passed the phone over to Paul, who struggled to find anything new to say.

"Yes," he confirmed. "Yes, it's still the mirrors, all the versions of her bad self, as she sees it... Well, perhaps that's what hell is, or indeed heaven. We are alone with ourselves. It seems very unfair, I agree..."

They chatted some more, and Paul wondered if he was right to sense greater warmth in Neve Cotter's voice. She had clearly not been impressed by him in the past, but since he had done his best to take the burden of Liz's torment from Ella, she had become kinder.

In another life, would I have asked her out for dinner and a movie? Paul wondered. *Well, guess I'll probably never know.*

Doctor Blume saw them out and bade them farewell as she locked up her office. The miserable weather had persisted into the November night, and Paul shivered as they dashed to Mike's car. In the distance, they heard shouting, a smash of glass. It was nearly two in the morning, but some locals were still outside, almost certainly drunk, and possibly fighting.

"Come to historic Tynecastle," said Mike as they buckled up. "Where the nightlife is noisy, copulatory, pukey, and has that edge of raw physical danger we can all enjoy."

"Oh, to be young again," smiled Paul. "If only they knew what's out there. Or what might be out there."

During the drive back to their shared house, they talked in a desultory fashion, of the Palmer entity. Strange events had been piling up since Paul had tried to destroy Rookwood, but there was no discernible pattern. They agreed, if Palmer was active, he was either playing a subtle game, or was just lashing out crazily.

"Could be a bit of both," added Mike, sourly.

Their conversation was interrupted by a sudden explosion, high above. It was a firework rocket, reminding Paul that tomorrow was November 5th.

"No," he said aloud. "No, it's today."

"Yep," Mike said, glancing up. "Bonfire night, AKA Guy Fawkes' Night, when we celebrate the fact that a 17th-century religious fanatic failed to blow up the King and Parliament, and then got burned at the stake along with his pals."

"These days, maybe some people feel he should be applauded for giving it a damn good try," observed Paul. "Do people still burn Guy Fawkes in effigy? I don't recall seeing that last year."

Mike shrugged as he turned onto the main expressway across town. Another rocket exploded, then a salvo of three or four sprayed red starbursts against the backdrop of low-hanging clouds.

"I doubt it," he said. "When I was very young, the older kids used to wheel a Guy through the streets. 'Penny for the Guy,' that was the old chant, but trick or treat on Halloween has replaced it."

Paul nodded, remembering how American the English Halloween had seemed, and how it almost coincided with the much older autumn bonfire festival. Another rocket exploded high above the streets, further away now, bangs fading to become sharp pops.

"I forgot to ask," said Mike, as he pulled into their street. "How's the tutelage going?"

"Oh God, don't ask," Paul groaned. "All these nightmare sessions are not doing anything for my concentration. But at least it brings in some cash. I just wish they'd stop asking me to write their essays for 'em."

"Entitled little brats," Mike said. "And here we are, home sweet home."

***

Farson finished up at the storage unit and drove the uniformed constable back to police headquarters. The young woman remarked on the inevitable fireworks that were being set off around the city.

"I hope none of these idiots blow their faces off," she said. "Or if they do, it's not on my shift."

"They should ban the damn things," said Farson. "Only professionals should handle things that go bang. Basic common sense."

They drove on in silence for another few minutes.

"Sir," the constable asked. "Do you think—something is going on?"

Farson glanced sideways at his subordinate.

"Something's always going on, Sue—that's why we still have work."

"That's not what I meant, sir," she said, irritably. "You know, like that bridge jumper, and this thing with the books. They're just weird. And all that business at the old asylum."

She hesitated, and Farson imagined her thought processes.

I'm Spooky Farson, I get all the odd cases nobody wants. But now there are so many, it's hard to make a joke of them, hard for the top brass to ignore, never mind the lower ranks.

"You can speak freely, Sue, if that's what you're worried about."

The woman took a deep breath.

"A lot of the guys down the nick, they think this Palmer stuff is becoming a real threat. There are so many mental cases, now, and we only see the ones that are a public safety threat. This friend of mine works at the infirmary, and she says the number of people with psychiatric problems has gone way up. Right across the board, no obvious explanation."

Farson had already observed this trend, but it was still interesting to find that others were seeing it, too.

"And," Sue continued, "there's this graffiti all over the place."

Farson frowned, not grasping the significance of the point. Seeing his expression, the young officer gestured at a derelict pub as they passed.

"You didn't see it, on the wall there?" she asked.

"I saw the usual spray-painted crap," he replied. "Why?"

"Take a closer look," she urged. "Next time you see a wall covered with tags and all that, look more closely."

They arrived at headquarters a few moments later, and Farson spent the next few hours filling out online forms. He tackled the suicide first, though he always found it the hardest subject to deal with, even including murder. He used the most detached jargon he could muster, distancing himself from the horror of a young life ended for no good reason.

"But maybe for a good reason this time," he muttered.

He checked the background details of the young woman. She had been a student at Tynecastle University, specializing in advanced software design. On a hunch, he Googled her name, and found she had been featured in her local newspaper as a star student, and had won a scholarship. He then chided himself for procrastination, because he hated the one duty he was bound to perform right now, tonight. He obtained her parents' home phone number, took a deep breath, and made the call.

The conversation was a long and difficult one.

***

Mike had been snoring next door for a couple of hours when Paul finally decided to go to bed. He had been trying to prepare notes for his online tutelage service, which he offered to history students around the world in return for meager amounts of cash. He had little chance of obtaining any kind of regular teaching post in the near future, given his notoriety. But, by concealing his identity, he had managed to build up an online clientele who did not think of him as 'the asylum guy'.

As usual, the messages from his clients ranged from intelligent questions to desperate pleadings for help. He skimmed through, flagging up queries he could deal with simply by sending a 'sample essay' or something similar. He wondered how many students would submit his work as their own, without altering a single word. Then he realized he was past caring, and very tired.

"I tell them not to cheat, they cheat anyway, the little bastards," he mumbled wearily as he slipped under his duvet.

He had hoped for a dreamless sleep, but instead, he kept waking from an uneasy slumber dogged by confusing images. He kept finding himself back at Rookwood, and the building was both the modern apartment complex he had known, and the Grim post-war asylum where Liz had been incarcerated. He relived Palmer's experiments on Liz and his other human guinea pigs. The death of Palmer and most of the inmates and staff in 1955 was somehow combined with Paul's own attempt to destroy the building. He felt the blast of his improvised bomb, the heat of the blaze on his skin. And he saw, once again, the Palmer entity reeling in the flames, apparently unable to escape the scene of the doctor's monstrous crimes.

"But you were wrong about that, weren't you?"

Paul opened his eyes to see a small, shadowy figure standing by his bed. The voice was familiar.

"Liz? Am I still dreaming?"

He could not see her face in the faint light from the curtained window, but made out a shrug.

"Why ask me?" she said. "I lost touch with reality a long time ago."

Paul sat up, reached out to try and take her hand. But Liz vanished as suddenly as she had appeared. He wondered if it had been a hallucination, or whether the girl had been present in some real sense.

One thing's for sure, he thought. *The old link between us is still there, and it may be getting stronger.*

This time, the sleep that came was deep and refreshing, utterly without dreams. The following morning Paul got up early and made breakfast for himself and Mike. He flipped on the local radio news from habit and heard about 'another tragic suicide of a Tyncastle University student'. He paused in pouring Mike's coffee and waited for more information.

"What's up?" Mike said blearily, walking slowly into the kitchen in an old t-shirt, boxers, and nothing else.

"Not your style quotient," Paul replied, and raised a finger for silence.

The radio newsreader confirmed the young woman had been studying at the 'university's world-class computer science department'. Questions were now being asked about whether students were under too much pressure in the highly competitive environment. Then the announcer moved on to the previous night's soccer results.

"If only we could put it down to pressure," said Mike. "And thanks, again, for my morning shot of caffeine."

"How many students is that?" Paul asked, pouring himself a cup. "Three? In a couple of months."

"The local suicide rate is up across the board, though," Mike pointed out. "Last week, there was that window cleaner. And that elderly couple in a suicide pact. The lorry driver who tried to take out the bus queue."

Paul nodded doubtfully. It was almost impossible to say what unpleasant incidents in or around Tynecastle might be down to the Palmer entity. And, as Palmer was no longer bound to the Rookwood site, it was not clear where the limits of his activity might be. Mike had even speculated that the monstrous gestalt being could go anywhere but was hanging around Tynecastle because it was familiar territory. Paul was dubious about that idea, given Palmer's massive egotism.

"But we can't be sure of anything except that the bugger survived," Mike concluded, before shoveling porridge into his mouth. "And we've no idea how to stop him, neutralize him, whatever."

Paul, munching toast, nodded again.

"If only there was an instruction manual for banishing—well, whatever the hell we're up against," Mike went on. "But it seems Palmer's a unique being."

"It's hard to believe that nothing like this has happened before," said Paul, taking out his frustration on some toast, which promptly disintegrated from vigorous buttering. "What about Percy's missing books? Palmer must have had a reason for destroying them."

Mike shrugged.

"Most of the ones that were ripped apart seemed to be about urban legends, hauntings, folklore linked to cities. They're all out there—some as ebooks, some second-hand. I've spent a small fortune on them. But there's one that doesn't seem to be available for love or money. Sod's Law says that might be the one we actually need."

Mike got up and went into the lounge, returned with a sheet of paper that had been heavily annotated in pen. Paul took it, skimmed the list of titles. One had been ringed in red.

"God, how do you even pronounce that?" he asked. "Sounds bonkers."

"Probably is bonkers," Mike said. "But it's also one of the rarest books on the planet. Not on Gutenberg or any of those other sites. Actual physical copies run to thousands of pounds, when they come on sale, which seems to be once in a blue moon."

Paul stared at the title and author, wondering if it might represent another blind alley in his long, uneven conflict with Palmer. It was a battle he had never wanted, and one he still had little idea of how to fight.

"I suppose we could contact rare book dealers rather than just rely on the web," he said.

Mike smiled, as he got up to put his bowl in the sink.

"Ahead of you, mate. Percy sometimes dealt with this guy in Durham, and I sent him an email asking if he knew the book. Preferably for a price that doesn't require me to take out a second mortgage."

"You think he'll have a copy of..." Paul peered at the list again. "And even if he doesn't, I guess he'll know how to pronounce it."

***

After talking to the dead girl's mother, Farson moved on to the death of Declan Mooney, which was less stressful, but more puzzling. He found no contact details for the dead man's relatives, and felt relief tinged with guilt. He went through some bagged evidence, mostly personal possessions, but saw nothing out of the ordinary. Then he moved on to the lock-up. The bookseller, Beynon, was clearly a meticulous man, as he had left a long list of his stored volumes pinned to the wall of the unit. Farson glanced at it, wondering idly how much second-hand books might fetch. Then he paused, looked again.

"Bloody hell."

He went onto the police force intranet and looked up a file that had been officially closed some time ago. It was the death of an elderly, retired academic, who had supposedly died during a botched home invasion. Farson had never liked the neat conclusion that some junkies broke in and tortured the poor old geezer, not least because of the very targeted way a dozen or so of the old man's books had been comprehensively shredded.

"He kept a list, too, as I recall…"

Sure enough, there was a jpg image of Lance Percival's book catalog, or at least one page of it. Farson compared it with the list from Beynon's storage unit and saw there was one title in common.

"Bingo!" he exclaimed, and heads turned.

"Yes, I'm playing online Bingo," he explained. "Any objections?"

The other officers and civilian staff returned to their work.

Farson went online to see if he could find out anything more about the book in question. He quickly established it was ludicrously rare. It was probably a dead end, he reasoned, but he could at least send an email to the book dealer about his destroyed and damaged property.

After he sent off the message, he was surprised by the general stir around him, then realized it was the end of the shift. He was about to put his jacket back on when he felt a niggling sense he had left something undone. He checked the various reports and messages he had written and saw nothing amiss. Then he picked up the pamphlet he had bagged and gazed at it for a few moments.

"Beynon," he said. "Unusual name. Have I heard it before?"

He made a records search and found two reports of break-ins at Beynon's premises, the most recent three years ago. Nobody had been charged. No way could such minor offenses have been noted by Farson. Then he found something else, a death in odd circumstances. It had happened nearly twelve years earlier, in Durham City. The body of a tattooist had been found dead in her shop, with no sign of a break-in. The coroner had recorded an open verdict, which was the official way of saying 'I've got no clue on this one.'

"Bingo!" hissed Farson.

Durham County detectives had found the tattooist's account book. It had shown she had spent dozens of hours on a job for an unnamed client who had always paid in cash. The mystery customer had been the last person to see her alive. A request for information had led to an anonymous tip-off, naming John Beynon as a frequent visitor. However, the book dealer had denied knowing the dead woman, and the lead officer on the case had considered it a case of mistaken identity.

"So that's two weird deaths, arguably," Farson said to himself as he logged out of the system. "Might be coincidence. Might not be."

It was still dark, of course, and the rain continued to dampen the city roads, and his spirits. As he drove home, he caught sight of graffiti-covered walls and remembered his conversation with the young constable.

"Okay," he murmured, pulling over under a railway viaduct, "let's have a look."

Farson took a torch and used it to study the chaotic swirls of sprayed color that obscured the Victorian brickwork. At first, he saw nothing unusual in the graffiti, just the usual mess of colors and shapes, enlivened in a couple of places by something that might have been art. Farson preferred the post-Impressionists and wondered—not for the first time—if anybody was taught to draw hands these days. But then he noticed what he took to be an odd symbol. It was painted in black, and seemed to be new, covering an older image.

Farson looked more closely, wondering if it was simply a tag. Then he saw the symbol again. Now that he was aware of it, he saw it was repeated dozens of times all across the archway of the viaduct. What's more, it looked as if more than one person had been responsible—there were differences in style and technique. But it was always the same cryptic knot of interwoven lines.

"So what?" he thought, and was about to get back into his car when the truth struck him. Far from being an abstract pattern, the much-repeated tag was simply a very stylized version of three letters.

M, R, and P. Miles Rugeley Palmer.

"Does he have a fan club now?" Farson murmured at the night as he resumed his journey to his home on the northernmost fringe of the city. "That's not a happy thought."

As he drove through the early rush hour traffic, he kept a lookout for more graffiti. Now that he knew what he was looking for, he saw the three intertwined letters again and again. After he had counted ten examples, he stopped counting.

He does have a fan club, the detective thought. *I shouldn't be surprised. Supposedly sane women want to marry serial killers on death row. Internet bigots deny the Holocaust. In a society that's going crazy in so many obvious ways, admiring Palmer is not the craziest thing someone might do.*

CHAPTER 2

Paul spent the morning working online, trying to help students who often seemed to be their own worst enemies. Mike had teaching until early afternoon. Halfway through the morning, he called to say he had had a reply from the bookdealer, who was keen to talk to them.

"We could drive over later today," Mike suggested.

"Yep, why not?" Paul said. "I could do with a change of scene. Just getting out of Tynecastle for a few hours sounds like a great idea."

After the call, Paul went back to his online tutelage. But, as often happened, he found himself being distracted. News alerts told him more about the suicide on the Tyne Bridge from the previous night. There was also a 'man found dead' story about a storage unit. The dead man had not been named, but Paul felt a stirring of curiosity and flagged the story for follow-ups.

Another one of his clients messaged him, asking for some facetime to discuss the impact of the American Civil War blockade on Britain's cotton industry. While this was well within Paul's realm of expertise, he had to refuse. He was determined nobody should link his carefully crafted profile on the tutelage site with the crazy guy who blew up a building.

'Sorry,' he typed back to bouncycastle111. 'I can only interact via direct messages on this site.'

There was a brief pause, then a sad face emoji appeared. He smiled, wondering whether most communication online would soon be in the form of cartoonish pictograms. He asked the student to outline their problems and promised to respond quickly.

Another potential source of income popped up. This one used the handle CindyCross008, and Paul wondered idly if the person's actual name was Cindy Cross. This time, there was no request for facetime, merely a general inquiry on the influence of Spiritualism on late nineteenth century society. This was uncomfortably close to the cause of all Paul's problems, but he put it down to coincidence.

'Not really my field of expertise,' he replied cautiously. 'What do you want to know?'

Soon, he was interacting with what he felt was probably a female student who seemed bright but troubled. From a few chance comments, he thought she might be at Tynecastle, and was under a lot of stress. He did not dare ask her outright, however. The tutelage site's rules dictated he should not ask any personal questions, and he knew that software could spot violations.

Despite his reservations, he soon found himself absorbed in an enjoyable discussion with CindyCross008. For the first time in months, he was able to think about his scholarly work and tried to impart ideas to an eager student. He realized how much he missed the predictable normality of teaching and wondered ruefully if he would ever get his career back on track.

By lunchtime, Paul's interrupted night was taking its toll on his concentration, and he had to sign out. He made himself a sandwich and tried to wake up with strong coffee. But, while waiting for Mike to return, he found himself mindlessly netsurfing, his thoughts inevitably straying toward all things Rookwood. A name flashed up in a sidebar. It made him stop and click on the title.

Great British Hauntings—Asylum of Fear!

Mia Callan's feature-length documentary on Rookwood was finally available to watch on-demand. He had forgotten the date, and that Mia had been annoyed she could not relaunch the series on Halloween. Weeks earlier, Paul had been offered the chance to view it, but decided against it. He moved the cursor over the thumbnail and saw a series of preview clips, including one of him speaking outside the gates of the apartment. He looked, he felt, more like an amiable dimwit than an outright lunatic. Then the scene cut to what was obviously news footage of the fire he had started. He contemplated a return to notoriety, being recognized whenever he left the house.

"Oh, God, maybe I should grow a beard."

The idea had originally been suggested half-seriously by Mike. Paul had rejected it, assuming people would easily see through such a basic change of image. But now he wondered if people were, by and large, inattentive enough to be fooled by the simple tactic. He went upstairs to the bathroom and looked in the mirror. He thought he might simply stop shaving for a few days and see how it went.

A shadow passed swiftly, a darkening of the dimly lit passage behind him. He spun around to look directly at nothing but an open door. Paul advanced cautiously out of the bathroom to gaze toward the top of the stairs. There was no further sign of movement.

"Mike?" he said loudly.

The house was well-heated, but as he walked toward the landing, he sensed a fall in temperature, as if a window had been left open somewhere. He paused, leaning on the banister, looking down in the hallway. The temperature gradually returned to normal.

"Liz?" he asked, more quietly.

No, he thought, *no way could she come back that easily.*

The sound of Mike's key in the front door was startling. Paul almost ran down the stairs, glad that another living human being was there.

***

John Beynon welcomed his visitors into the small flat he occupied above his shop. He sized them up carefully and concluded they were genuine in their interest in the book. Which raised interesting questions that Beynon kept to himself.

"Tea?" he asked. "No? You don't mind if I indulge? I pretty much survive on tea, biscuits, the odd bit of fruit."

Mike Bryson, the friend of Lance Percival, admired the view from the living room window. The American, Paul Mahan, seemed preoccupied but looked out at the cathedral and made an appropriate noise.

"Yes, Durham is blessed with one of the finest examples of Norman architecture," Beynon said, swirling the contents of his teapot. "But one grows blasé about the view. See something beautiful every day and soon it's little more than wallpaper. Human beings can become habituated to anything."

The visitors settled on the couch and waited while Beynon poured himself a cup of Darjeeling. Then he sat opposite them, and the real business of the meeting began.

"Now," he said, smiling. "You're interested in Thibaut de Castries' notorious book of modern occultism. I won't ask why—your fame has preceded you, Mr. Mahan. I saw that rather sensational television show, Great British Hauntings. You came across rather well, I thought."

"Thanks," said the American, "and, please, call me Paul."

"I'm Mike," put in Bryson.

"Of course, and you must call me John," said Beynon. "Formality is out of place among true booklovers, I feel. I was always on first-name terms with poor Lance. And you say that his copy of *Megapolisomancy* was deliberately destroyed? Extraordinary."

"I believe it was the Palmer entity, as we call it," Mahan said.

Beynon noted the man's tiredness and anxiety. He wondered if the American's mental health was holding up. Mahan didn't look as if he was capable of blowing up an apartment building. He looked, in fact, like a washed-out history lecturer. But Beynon had met a lot of strange people down the years and knew better than to judge by appearances.

"Palmer, yes," Beynon said carefully. "Kind of paramental, judging by Mike's description."

Seeing their puzzlement, he smiled and gestured with his teaspoon.

"The cathedral out there—do you think it's haunted?"

Mahan looked puzzled, shrugged.

"There must be ghost stories related to such an old building," Bryson remarked. "But Palmer is something different, you do get that?"

"Precisely!"

Beynon stood and started pacing, still waving his teaspoon. He knew he cut a slightly absurd figure but did not mind if he was seen as a harmless eccentric. Besides, he could think more effectively on the move.

"The traditional ghost," he continued, "is a single person—the headless horseman or the weeping nun, or a murdered stable boy. Whether they are real or not, we think of these entities as unique individuals. But these old-fashioned ghosts—assuming they exist at all, of course—come from a rather different world than ours. A world of simple, agrarian communities, small cities, a pre-technological society."

He paused and saw curiosity but no obvious understanding in his visitors' expressions.

"Now," he went on, "consider the modern world, a world of huge cities, of billions of people, of massive energy sources, and instant communications. Vast agglomerations of people, energy, paper, steel, plastic, glass, and, of course, information. Our peasant ancestors would view the modern city as miraculous and terrifying. The fact that we do not find our cities astonishing ought to concern us, I feel, and so did de Castries. The world of social media and terrorism and climate change is far from the old, slow-moving, quaint world of the old-school ghost. No, if one accepts the central premise of *Megapolisomancy*, the modern world is far more likely to be haunted by paramental entities!"

"Okay," said Mahan, rubbing his eyes. "I'll bite. What are paramentals?"

Beynon continued pacing, excited to be sharing thoughts he had pondered deeply for so many years.

"According to Thibaut de Castries, paramentals are beings created exclusively by modern, urban conditions. They are not individuals in the sense of the old-school ghost, but composite beings compounded of many elements. They are not merely the surviving essence of a dead person, but also fragmentary elements of modern life in general—the despair of the impoverished, the rage of the gangster, the fear of the victim. Thus, a whole array of different personalities might be blended with the general atmosphere of the city to create what seems to be a single entity. Hence the title of his book—*Megapolisomancy*—the magic of huge cities."

"Are you sure," Bryson asked, "that de Castries was talking about beings like Palmer? I mean, this Frenchman could just have been an old crank who wrote a book full of self-indulgent twaddle."

Beynon had to laugh at that. Bryson, at first impression, seemed rather amiable and shallow, but he recalled Percival saying the 'lad', whom he had taught many years ago, was a clear thinker.

"Occultists are rather prone to 'twaddle', as you put it," Beynon said tactfully. "And de Castries seems to have spent some time as a member of the famous Order of the Golden Dawn, who were notoriously keen on obscure mysticism. But some claim that, after he split with them, old Thibaut did manage to conjure up a paramental of his own. A veiled woman supposedly accompanied him throughout his later life. This woman's face was allegedly seen just once, by an errand boy who stumbled into de Castries apartment when the door was left ajar. The boy went insane and could never describe what he saw. Or so the story goes."

Bryson and Mahan looked at one another. Mahan shrugged.

"Okay, that's a nice anecdote," the American said. "But this veiled woman still doesn't sound much like Palmer. I've fought against that gestalt entity, and it doesn't retain a consistent form. It shifts and is often invisible."

"I know!" said Beynon. "Isn't it fascinating? According to de Castries, most paramentals are relatively weak, mindless, and quite unstable. This means they don't last long. De Castries likens the minor paramentals to fashion trends and crazes in modern urban life, spectacular for a short while. But, sometimes, a really powerful one appears and can endure."

"Could you give us just one example?" Bryson put in. "Because, again, de Castries seems to want us to take a lot on trust."

"Jack the Ripper," replied Beynon.

"Aw, come on!" Mahan protested.

But they're intrigued, Beynon thought. *If I sell this bit well, they're hooked.*

"Think about it," he said slowly. "A violent, destructive force, specifically targeting women who were victims of a hypocritical, chaotic society. Witnesses described a bewildering array of possible suspects, ranging from gentlemen in top hats to skulking maniacs, and even female killers. Was the Ripper a toff, a copper, a midwife? And why was it so hard to catch a homicidal maniac in such a small area of a densely populated city? Perhaps it was because, like Palmer, Red Jack was a composite being, an unusually strong paramental produced by the many evils of Victorian society, fueled by terror, but ultimately too unstable to endure."

Mahan looked skeptical, but Bryson nodded, evidently impressed, and asked another question.

"Does that mean the Palmer entity will fade away? If nothing is done to fuel it, feed it?"

"I suspect so," Beynon said carefully. "But it is being fed, isn't it? Even I know Palmer has won global attention, and many seem to admire him. Shocking, I know, but Hitler and Stalin also have their fans nowadays, do they not?"

"Okay," Mahan said, "I admit this is all somewhat plausible. But I still think Palmer is in a different league to these paramentals."

"Possibly," Beynon said in a placatory tone. "But de Castries was right about another key point. He wrote that these new, dark gods tend to devour older, simpler pagan deities. Which explains how the Palmer entity came to be and absorbed the old god of Rookwood. What's more, de Castries claimed to be a sorcerer who could command more powerful paramentals. He hinted he was responsible for the 1906 San Francisco earthquake."

Beynon paused his talk and stopped pacing, waiting for his guests' reactions.

"I guess you read this in your copy of de Castries' book?" asked Mahan, his expression suddenly keen and alert.

Sharper than I thought, Beynon noted. *I'll have to watch him. Both of them.*

"No, I'm afraid I read the copy I sold to my old friend Lance," Beynon said with a rueful smile. "Sadly, I'm speaking from memory. You will find a lot of guff on the internet from people who claim to have read de Castries, but the truth is there are only three or four copies of *Megapolisomancy* left in the entire world. The print run was limited, and there were no further editions."

The discussion continued, with Beynon explaining de Castries had been born in France around 1870, but nobody was quite sure. He certainly ended up in San Francisco sometime before the great earthquake of 1906. He then seemed to vanish from the historical record, but some say he died around 1930.

"And his book," Mahan said. "It was descriptive, it outlined his theories—but did it give any instructions on how to control or destroy paramentals? Because we're in a war here, not holding a symposium."

"Straight to the point!" Beynon exclaimed. "Very good. So far as I can recall, it does not."

Seeing his guests' reaction, he quickly elaborated.

"But know your enemy is surely one of the great principles of strategy, is it not?" he asked. "The better we understand the Palmer entity, the more likely we are to find its weakness and defeat it."

"We?" echoed the American. "Are you offering to join us, fight the good fight?"

Suspicious, and rightly so, Beynon thought. *But they are both keen to recruit a knowledgeable ally, which they can see I am. Bryson might sway his more skeptical friend. Especially if I deliver the goods.*

"If you want my help locating the book, and nothing more, then we will treat it purely as a business arrangement," he said brightly. "But really, you describe such a monstrous threat to innocent lives—isn't it my duty, as a concerned citizen, to try and do more?"

***

"What do you think?" asked Mike, as they wended their way out of the side streets, back toward the parking lot. "Apart from the obvious remarks about English eccentrics."

Paul mulled over his feelings about John Beynon. The actual bookshop, with its over-filled shelves, was the real deal. He could imagine Lance Percival spending many a happy hour just browsing there. But he wondered if Mike's old friend would have counted Beynon as more than a mere acquaintance.

"How well did Percy know him?" he asked. "And did he trust him?"

Mike looked puzzled, as if he had never considered the question.

"Well, he was on the old guy's list of contacts—which he kept in an address book," he said. "As for trust, he never said he'd been overcharged. But suppose you're right to infer it was more of a business connection than a friendship. Why? Don't you like him? I got that vibe."

"You don't think," Paul asked, "he might be another Max Rodria? Someone so high on his own cleverness that he won't listen to anyone else? Because that does not end well. And there's another thing."

Paul looked up at the Cathedral, standing solidly on its rocky eminence, nine hundred years old, and a perfect symbol of continuity. He gestured at it.

"Sometimes, you just get a feeling about a person, or a place, or a building," he said. "I like that big old church of yours—it's not too pretty, but it has a kind of aura, you feel it's a good place. By contrast, I felt uneasy the whole time we were in Beynon's place, like we were being watched by someone. Or something…"

They dodged around a group of noisy girls emerging from a pub, then Paul spoke again.

"Did Beynon's flat strike you as cold?" he asked.

"No, not especially," Mike said, again looking quizzical.

"So, why was he wearing a long-sleeved turtleneck? A couple of times, he actually pulled the sleeves down and the collar up. It seemed unconscious, kind of a mannerism. That was one definite thing that bothered me."

They had reached the parking lot, and Mike was fumbling for his keys.

"I suppose," he said, unlocking his car. "I suppose the actual shop is a bit chilly this time of year. Maybe he simply feels the cold; the bloke must be at least sixty, maybe older."

Paul made a noncommittal noise, unconvinced, but unable to argue against a sensible argument. As Mike reversed out of the parking space, Paul glanced in the side mirror to his left, and shouted a warning. Mike stopped the car with a jerk as Paul twisted around in his seat.

"What is it?" Mike asked.

"I thought I saw someone—a woman. She was right behind—at least I think..."

Paul trailed off, rubbed his eyes.

"Maybe you should have a nap when we get back," Mike said, gesturing at the dash. "I'd have seen someone behind us, wouldn't I?"

Paul looked at the small screen mounted just inches away. Of course, Mike would not have been so careless, especially not with so many people around. It was probably weariness and stress making his senses unreliable. Fragments of his nightmares might well have been bleeding into his waking imagination.

"You're not seeing ghosts again, are you?" Mike asked, mild irritation giving way to concern. "I thought that had worn off."

"It had—it has worn off, I'm sure," Paul assured him. "I'd know if that unwanted gift was coming back, believe me. No, you're probably right, I could have just imagined it."

Mike maneuvered carefully into the traffic, swearing under his breath as more groups of students scurried across the narrow street.

"They think they live charmed lives, the young," he growled as another jaywalker dodged in front. "There should be some kind of training course for all teenagers, where they learn what it feels like to be hit by a small motor vehicle. That would make the little buggers think twice."

Paul laughed at the very British sourness of the remark. Then the image of a car crash naturally recalled the moment when he had driven Mike's old car into the East Wing of Rookwood and triggered his makeshift bomb. He saw again the Palmer entity rising up from the flames, a monster of electrical cables, shattered brickwork, broken glass, and other debris. The absorption of the old pagan god of Rookwood was finally achieved in a fiery chaos that he, Paul, had recklessly created. Then another thought struck him, something Beynon had said.

"Just a goddamn minute!" he exclaimed. "How did he know Palmer absorbed the old god?"

Mike looked confused.

"Didn't you talk about it when—at the hearing, when you..."

"When a judge decided I was too batshit crazy to go to jail for arson?" Paul said. "No, I didn't. So far as I recall, that whole aspect of the situation isn't common knowledge."

Mike looked dubious, and Paul realized his friend did not want to state the obvious. Paul had probably been jabbering all sorts of wild ideas to police, firefighters, paramedics, and others after he was arrested on that fateful night. Word could easily have gotten out.

"Well," Mike said finally, "let's check online. If it's on the web, it's common knowledge. Someone like Beynon would definitely be keeping up with weird local events."

"And reading the comments, yeah, I get that," said Paul glumly. "You're probably right. But I'm gonna check."

They reached the outskirts of Durham City, and Paul noticed a huge bonfire in a public park. Technicians in bright orange jackets were swarming around the area. Paul guessed they were setting up one of the dozens of official fireworks displays that would erupt across the area in the early evening.

Paul's phone chimed, and he checked it, frowning. The man calling had not had occasion to talk to him for months.

***

John Beynon watched his visitors until they walked around the corner and vanished from view. Then he closed the curtains, switched on a small reading lamp, and went to a locked cabinet behind the sagging sofa. From the cabinet, he took two books, laid them on a low table next to his half-empty teacup.

One book was a dog-eared, printed volume, with pages that had been expertly glued back onto the spine several times by its owner. The second was smaller, much thinner, and when Beynon opened its worn and cracked black cover, he revealed handwritten pages on unlined paper. He turned a page and stopped to peer closely at a bewildering array of diagrams and other vaguely algebraic-looking formulae.

"Well, that was a rewarding meeting," he said, "for me, at least."

He flipped through the handwritten book and settled on a page that combined written text and diagrams. Beynon's mouth began to move as he mouthed a series of syllables, pausing occasionally to gaze around the room. After several minutes, he fell silent and sat back in his well-worn armchair. A slight displacement of air rustled the pages of the open book. Beynon smiled at the indistinct figure that formed in the far corner, a roughly human shape congealing out of the shadows.

"You took your time, missy," he commented, his tone mildly reproving. "But you can still catch them if you move quickly. Observe, assess, report. But don't be detected by you-know-who."

There was a flickering darkness, like the sudden shadow of a bird passing overhead on a bright day. Then the spectral form was gone. Beynon shuddered slightly, breath clouding the air in front of his face as he wrapped his thin arms around himself. The gesture caused a sleeve to ride up, revealing a dense tattoo pattern on the old man's wrist. He pulled the garment down quickly. It was a reflex action. He did not think anyone was watching, even in these days of spy cameras and the like. But he was in the habit of concealment.

Next, Beynon replaced the black journal in his locked cabinet. He went back to his armchair and picked up the larger book, flipped through it, shaking his head at certain passages. It had nothing new to teach him, but was still entertaining, in its way.

I'll let them wait a while, he thought, *then tell them I've achieved the almost impossible, and charge them a perfectly reasonable price for the damn thing into the bargain. Say, three hundred. No, two-fifty. It's not as if I need the money.*

Chuckling, he set down his well-thumbed copy of *Megapolisomancy: A New Science of Cities* and went into his small kitchen to start preparing his evening meal.

CHAPTER 3

"Afternoon, sir," said one of the armed policemen flanking the doorway.

As Whins passed by the uniformed pair, he listened carefully for a titter, or some satirical comment. He detected no sign of disrespect. But he could not hear their thoughts, and he knew that, for many people, he was essentially the punchline to a tasteless joke.

The Honorable George Brockley Whins had lost his place in the government eight months earlier due to a sex scandal. His wife had left him, his grown-up children shunned him, and one tabloid had dubbed him 'Bi-Curious George'. That last one had stung a little, not least because of its accuracy. But what hurt the politician most was the loss of status, his exile from any real political power.

Whins had only been a junior minister at the Defense Department, but before being forced to resign, he had been on a definite upward track. He was sure he was destined to be prime minister, with a mission to restore Britain to its former greatness. Whins had never been too clear on how he was going to achieve that. But he had absolute confidence in his own abilities to do pretty much anything.

Today, November 5th, he was striding purposefully out of the Palace of Westminster, home of the Parliament of the United Kingdom. A debate was scheduled for the afternoon, but he had no interest in housing policy. He was heading back to his constituency in the north, to occupy himself with more serious matters than the plight of homeless riffraff.

Whins passed a statue of Churchill, and once again felt he shared the war leader's qualities. Churchill, after all, had been called a crank, shunned by his own party, and driven into the political wilderness by lesser men. Then he came to a statue of Oliver Cromwell, England's only military dictator.

Ah, the real deal, Whins thought. *If they don't do as they're told, shoot 'em, or chop their heads off.*

Whins smiled to himself at the thought of executing his many enemies, on all sides of the House and beyond. He had a list of reporters and news editors who had piled on the misery during the weeks when the scandal unfolded. As he hailed a cab, he pondered the various ways he might slowly torture such vermin to death.

"Where to, mate?" asked the cabbie.

"King's Cross," replied Whins. "I've got a train to catch. People to meet."

One person in particular, he thought. *My special advisor.*

He sank back in the rear seat and pondered his new strategy. It was risky, some might say insane. But he had given up on the conventional, slow-track route to power. He was ready to try something unusual, something bizarre. And he didn't really mind who got hurt in the process, just so long as it wasn't him.

You can't make an omelet without breaking a few eggs, after all.

"Going north, then?" asked the driver. "Long journey. And they never seem to get the bloody trains running on time."

"One day, I will," Whins murmured.

***

The Strawberry was a traditional pub that had been revamped a little, but its proximity to Tyncastle's soccer ground meant it retained a hard-drinking, raucous character. Paul had only visited the place a couple of times and wondered why Farson wanted to meet there.

"Because it's not a police pub," Farson said simply, putting down his half-empty pint. "Some boozers are patronized by other members of the force. This one isn't. Here, I'm just another drinker, unless someone recognizes me. Which is just an occupational hazard, nothing we can do about that."

Paul and Mike pulled up two low stools and put their drinks on the small, round table. The Strawberry was half empty at six-thirty, and so far, they had attracted no curious glances. Paul reflected that they were close enough to Tynecastle University to run into lecturers or students.

"I should really grow that beard," he said to himself.

Farson looked at him oddly, then laughed.

"I get it, you get recognized more often than me," said the detective. "Well, I owe you an apology. I took you for a crank at first, then a nutcase. Now, I think you're right. Something bloody strange is going on in this town. Now, shall we order some food? Because this place will be heaving in half an hour."

Ten minutes later Farson explained why he had asked for the meeting. The death of Declan Mooney came as an unpleasant surprise to the friends.

"We couldn't find any next of kin, sadly," said Farson, "so we're going to release his name tomorrow, see if anyone gets in touch. Thought I'd give you a heads up. It's an odd coincidence, if that's what it is. And then there's the destruction of rare books—almost identical to what happened to your friend, Lance Percival."

"Whose books were they?" asked Paul, feeling almost sure he knew the answer.

"A guy in Durham called Beynon," replied Farson, then paused to study his listeners. "And my highly-trained detection skills tell me the name is familiar. Tell me more."

The conversation took a new, more exciting turn. Farson, after some hesitation, shared his suspicions about Beynon's past. Paul and Mike, in turn, talked about their meeting with him, and their common interest in *Megapolisomancy*. This led to a somewhat garbled attempt to explain de Castries' ideas, as conveyed by Beynon.

"Cities generate evil spirits?" Farson said, gazing out at the street. "Yeah, I can believe that. And I can believe this Palmer entity wants to curb everyone's knowledge of what it is, where its power lies. But you'll appreciate, in my line of work, I'm supposed to deal with boring, material evidence, not believe in the supernatural. Ah, here comes the grub at last."

Their food arrived, drinks were replenished, and speculation continued. Despite the increasing hubbub in the pub, exploding fireworks from a nearby riverside display were occasionally audible. Eventually, Farson put a proposal to Mike and Paul.

"I want to open a kind of shadow investigation in the whole Rookwood thing," he explained. "I'll be treating you two as confidential informants, which means I don't have to report any meetings. And, to keep things straight, I'll pay you the going rate—not much, but I'm guessing at least one of you could do with the cash?"

"Too right," said Paul, ruefully. "And thanks. So, what's our next move?"

"Carry on comparing notes, keep an eye on Beynon," the detective replied. "He hasn't actually lied. One of my colleagues informed him his property had been destroyed. It is odd, though, he didn't mention it to you. Not necessarily suspicious, just peculiar. From what I've gleaned, he's an odd fish, and you're right to be cautious. Now, as to Palmer... Hang on, is that me?"

It took a moment to establish that the repeating ringtone was Farson's phone. He gave up trying to hear the caller and signaled he was going outside to take it. As soon as he was out of sight, Paul and Mike had their own discussion. They decided to share more information, but only when they had arranged a more private meeting.

When Farson returned, however, he only did so to say he had to leave at once.

"Something's up," he said simply. "It seems to be a lot more than the usual bonfire night idiocy. They're calling in reinforcements. Something crazy's going on."

***

"There are some very small children here," said Ella Cotter, looking disapprovingly at a family group walking by. "Little kids will be scared by all the loud bangs."

"Some people haven't got much common sense," Neve said to her daughter, leaning down so she could speak quietly, "but maybe commenting on that fact too loudly would also be a bit unwise?"

Ella looked up at her mother, and Neve was pleased to see an actual smile appear on the slightly pinched, pale face. She reached down and tucked a strand of Ella's auburn hair under her woolly hat. The crowd heading into the park flowed around them, a mass of faces, smaller figures wielding multi-colored glow sticks, people of all sizes eating hot dogs, chips, or imbibing soft drinks.

"Let's get nearer the boating lake," Neve suggested. "Then we'll see all the fancy stuff going on at ground level."

They tried to weave their way to the railings that surrounded the diminutive lake, but the crowd was already four or five deep. Ella looked resigned rather than disappointed, and Neve asked if she would rather just go home and watch TV.

"No," said the girl, "we've come all this way, we might as well make a night of it."

Neve couldn't help smiling. Since Paul had intervened, with the help of Doctor Blume, Ella had slept more peacefully. The daughter she knew, by turns solemn and playful, had been restored to her. Neve's only worry was that Liz would return, as she had before. But tonight, they could simply enjoy the fireworks.

"Look, the bonfire!" Ella shouted, pointing, visibly excited for the first time.

A huge, conical heap of wood was being set ablaze a few yards away. There were desultory cheers from the onlookers as the fire caught hold, and orange flames licked hungrily at what appeared to be broken-up furniture and other debris. Soon a great column of flame was casting a lurid light over the still-growing crowd.

"They used to roast chestnuts on bonfires," Neve said. "But it's not allowed now."

"That's because of health and safety precautions," Ella pointed out. "And there are roasted chestnuts, I saw a stand on the way in."

"A subtle hint, well done," Neve smiled. "Shall we get some before they—"

Her sentence was interrupted by the whoosh of a rocket, which was followed by a loud bang. Neve checked her phone. It was seven pm, and the display was starting dead on time. More rockets rose from the far side of the little lake, exploding into a flower-like array of multicolored sparks. Some people oo-ed and ah-ed. Then a series of louder explosions erupted above them, fireworks shot from mortars producing what looked like showers of glowing jewels.

A small child began to cry loudly, its young parents failing to placate it with comforting words.

"I told you," Ella said.

"You certainly did," Neve admitted, as the family group moved off.

The next explosion was even louder, and Neve felt the shockwave, covered her ears. Glowing fragments fell among the crowd. Then a rocket shot across the lake, just clearing the heads of the adult onlookers, and flew out of the park to explode against the side of a house.

This time the screams came from all ages. Some people ducked, many began to move back from the fence at the lake's edge. The next rocket skimmed the shimmering water and bounced off a stocky man, who flailed his arms in the air, fell onto his back. The rocket shot wildly around, spraying golden sparks between people's feet, before exploding with deafening intensity just a few yards away.

"Mummy!" Ella cried, clutching at Neve's side.

Neve gripped her daughter's hand more tightly and started to flee. Ahead of them, at the main gates, a disorderly throng struggled to get out of the park. Neve could hear above the screaming and shouting an amplified voice urging everyone to remain calm. The speaker himself sounded scared, stammering his words, convincing no one. Behind Neve, there was a huge explosion, followed by screams of pain, not panic.

I've got to get her out, Neve thought.

"Don't look round!" she urged Ella. "Stay close."

"But, Mummy, look! It's the bad man again!"

Ella was pointing back toward the bonfire, her face distorted by terror. Neve turned and froze. The heap of wood waste was ablaze, a great column of fire and smoke reaching thirty or so feet into the November night. At first, she could not understand why Ella was so terrified. Then she saw it. In the flames, a face was forming, vanishing, appearing again. The features were only intermittently visible, but they were still instantly recognizable to mother and daughter. Eyes devoid of compassion gazed out from behind small, round spectacles, while a smile formed on a thin-lipped mouth beneath an old-fashioned mustache.

"Palmer!"

The shout had come from a young man standing nearby, and was taken up by others in the crowd. A whistling noise passed overhead, and then a firework exploded among the people thronging the gate. Bright-colored trails of sparks arced into the night air amid agonized cries of the wounded and terrified. The face in the flames smiled thinly and disappeared. Neve decided to get away from the crowd and urged Ella to run with her into a nearby clump of trees. Flashing lights and sirens showed help was arriving.

"We just have to wait here," Neve told her daughter, crouching down to hold the girl close. "Let's be very quiet and wait for help to come."

"Yes," said Ella, her voice calmer now. "That's the sensible thing to do."

How could Palmer do that? Neve wondered, clutching Ella to her damp overcoat. *Come to think of it, why would he? Okay, he could mess with the fireworks, but to manifest himself in flames—is he trying to become some kind of modern-day version of the Devil?*

She looked through the foliage at the bonfire and saw the column of fire was just that—a regular blaze. There was no trace of Palmer's visage. While people were still shouting and screaming, there was less obvious panic. Neve heard other voices giving orders, offering reassurance, telling people they would be okay.

"He's gone," Ella said, looking up at her mother. "He's gone away again."

"Yes," Neve agreed.

But where did he go?

***

By the time Farson got to the nearest crisis, the incident was over. He tried to find out what exactly had happened, but got garbled accounts from other officers, paramedics, and witnesses. Eventually, someone showed him a video recorded with their phone.

"It was a face," the woman insisted. "There was a face in the flames, just for a few seconds. And when it disappeared, the fireworks stopped."

Farson referred the woman to a harassed constable who was trying to take contact details. A white-faced man was introduced to him by another detective as the 'the chief fireworks bloke'. The man instantly corrected the officer and insisted in a loud voice he was a *pyrotechnician.*

"Well, it's a pity you're not a better one," shouted a bystander.

Farson led the man away from the confused and angry crowd to a squad car for questioning. Initially, the pyrotechnician was defensive, but when Farson hinted he knew something strange had happened, the man opened up.

"It was impossible, what happened," said the expert. "The mortars just swiveled forward and started firing at people. Rockets, too. It makes no sense. These things are fixed down solidly. And they can only be triggered electronically, from a central control panel. But nothing I did could stop them from firing!"

Farson told the man he was not to blame.

"It can't be your fault," the detective explained. "Because it's happening all over the city."

The pyrotechnician stared at Farson, then looked out at the flashing lights, teams of uniformed men and women trying to help the injured and traumatized. Then he looked back at the detective, lip trembling, tears starting to trickle down his face.

"All over?" he said weakly. "Why?"

***

"What's Palmer's game plan? I just don't get it."

"Me neither, Mike," said Paul. "It seems like he's out to create as much mayhem as possible."

They were back home, sitting in front of the TV, watching the BBC's rolling news coverage of the 'bonfire night carnage' in Tynecastle. It was already dominating the national news, and judging by the internet reactions, there was global interest, too. Mike looked up from his tablet and groaned as the announcer mentioned a familiar name.

"Oh, not that wanker again," said the Englishman. "The last thing we need is a politician's opinion on this."

Paul was inclined to agree. George Brockley Whins summed up everything he disliked about the British class system. Born to wealth and privilege, the man clearly loved the sound of his own voice and had a severely defective moral compass.

"I'll turn him off," Paul said.

The interviewer was asking Whins for his reaction to 'the night's shocking events'.

"Well, they may be deeply shocking," the MP replied, "but for me, they are not surprising."

Mike and Paul both fell silent, and Paul lowered the remote as Whins was asked what he meant.

"It's not exactly a secret that this city has become the focus of some very disturbing events in recent times," Whins said, pompously. "And before you ask, yes, I am talking about the old Rookwood Asylum. I know it is conventional wisdom to describe what happened there as a series of disconnected incidents, much of the evidence for the paranormal as fake or otherwise questionable. But, after carefully considering the issue, I think something much darker and more disturbing is happening."

The local BBC interviewer seemed to struggle to find her next question.

"Are you—are you saying you think the supernatural is involved in what's happened tonight?"

"I've seen the evidence, the same videos that you have watched," Whins said, looking pleased with himself. "Could all that be faked? We're talking time-stamped mobile phone footage from a dozen or more independent sources, all ordinary people who were just out to enjoy Guy Fawkes' Night with family and friends."

Whins looked away from the interviewer, gazed directly into the camera, unblinking.

"I would genuinely like to believe there is a mundane explanation for the face in the flames. I would love to have someone explain how so many carefully organized fireworks parties could all go wrong within minutes of each other. But I think we know it's gone beyond official explanations that, in fact, explain nothing. There has been a coverup of what happened at Rookwood, and now the evil is out there, unconstrained, and—as we heard in your last news update—at least one person has been killed."

The interviewer tried to ask another question, but Whins raised a meaty hand and plowed on.

"The time has come for those of us who want the truth to stand up and be counted. I intend to raise the question in Parliament, as is my right, and I will also be submitting written questions to the Home Secretary and the intelligence services. The people of this city have a right to know what kind of unnatural menace is threatening them, their families, and their homes."

The interviewer jumped in hastily to say they were out of time and had to cut back to the studio in London. Paul cut the broadcast. There was a long silence. Then Mike said what they were both thinking.

"That was a prepared speech. That slippery bastard knew this was going to happen."

They sat in silence for a few more moments before Mike spoke.

"If somebody who's fairly close to the government knows the score, maybe this is about preparing the public for a big revelation. Or maybe Whins is just using inside information to boost his public profile, and somebody in power will be really pissed off with him?"

"Well, whatever the truth, it really sucks the big one," Paul declared. "I mean, being on the same side as any politician would be bad enough, let alone that guy."

"Look on the bright side," Mike said, hesitantly. "Perhaps this will mean something will get done. I mean, something official."

Paul shook his head in disbelief.

"You think the paranormal version of MI5 will turn up and zap Palmer with some amazing James Bond-type gizmo? Makes a good movie plot, sure, but in real life?"

Mike raised his hands in a defensive gesture.

"Hey, shoot me for looking on the bright side for a change. But yeah, maybe there is some secret defense agency that deals with weird stuff. You never know."

Paul checked the time, sighed, and stood up.

"We should be getting ready," he pointed out. "Traffic looks to be crazy tonight, and we need to get to Blume's place before midnight."

Mike sighed as he levered himself upright.

"No peace for the wicked."

"You don't need to stay, you know," Paul pointed out. "You can drop me at Doc Blume's place, I'll get a taxi back."

Mike smiled, shook his head pityingly.

"Nope. You're stuck with me, pal," he insisted. "I can't let you out of my sight for too long, you might try to destroy another large building."

Paul felt his face redden but had to smile at his friend's genuine concern. Mike was far more nervous than he let on about the dream experiment with Ella and Liz. He was prepared to lose hours of sleep rather than not be around to help, if help were needed.

"Thanks," Paul said simply, then noticed that Mike was looking past him, frowning. "What is it?"

Mike went to the window and looked out at the street, then turned around appearing mildly worried.

"Probably nothing. I just thought I saw someone looking in the window. Not easy, they'd have had to sprint away and jump the garden wall in about two seconds. If they were a mere mortal, that is."

Paul felt a slight chill run up his spine, but then reasoned they were both jumpy and it might mean nothing.

"Could have been the ghost of Guy Fawkes," he suggested.

CHAPTER 4

"We got likes galore," said Laura Blaine. "Bloody hell, we'll have a hundred thousand by midnight at this rate. It's gone global! And people are paying to watch it. We could actually be making something above minimum wage. I think I might faint from excitement."

Mia Callan looked at the screen over her colleague's shoulder, made a noncommittal sound. Laura stood up to stretch, glanced out the window. With the editing suite in near darkness, she could see the last fireworks expiring in the cloudy skies over London, while a few ragged columns of bonfire smoke unraveled in the cold night breeze.

"We could have pulled the video at the last minute," Mia said. "They're sure to call it exploitation, all this stuff going on in Tynecastle—and that massive wanker Whins cashing in. We'll be linked to him, too. God, it's a mess. I'm not sure I understand what's happening, but we're exploiting it."

Laura, seated again at her desk, looked up at her boss, her expression puzzled.

"I know, I know," Mia went on. "You did a great job editing, and it's a good, solid piece of work. But this has gone beyond entertainment, or infotainment for that matter. Now I get the feeling that all we're doing is drumming up fans for Palmer, not for our next show—if we get to make one. Paul was right—that monster craved fame and power all his life, now he's getting it in death."

"Come on, Mia," Laura said. "If we didn't release the damn thing, the money men would have pulled the plug on *Great British Hauntings*, right? No more series, no more creative freedom. We'd have to go back to corporate stuff; commercials, god knows what."

Mia nodded, ran a hand through her short, blue-dyed hair.

"I know, but we've made a devil's bargain—creative freedom in return for publicizing something truly evil. Dangerous. Going back to making training films for blue chip companies might not be virtuous, but it might be the lesser evil..."

Laura said nothing more, and the pair silently watched the likes and comments roll in. It was a tremendous success, but Laura's initial exhilaration wore off, and she wondered just how many of the commenters were now ardent admirers, or even disciples, of Doctor Miles Rugeley Palmer.

***

Tonight, Doctor Blume—small, dark, and slender—seemed almost overwhelmed by the solid, traditional furnishings of her own office. She was clearly very nervous and seemed hesitant about resuming what Mike called 'our adventures in the realms of the bonkers'. When Paul asked her if she had doubts about continuing, she admitted that the night's events had disturbed her.

"We are on the edge of Palmer's world every time I put you under," she pointed out. "He seems particularly active now. Surely it must have occurred to you that he could seek you out in your dreams as easily as you are doing with Liz?"

Paul laid back on the well-upholstered couch, pondering the question, but before he could frame an answer Mike spoke up.

"Doc, what choice has he got? He can't abandon Ella to Liz. Whether the kid gets dragged down, or Liz possesses her, it's morally unacceptable either way."

Paul smiled up at the doctor.

"You heard the man," he said. "Send me into hell. I'm a big, damn hero."

The process was now simple and almost felt routine. Paul relaxed, listening to the therapist's voice as she took him to a place of comfort and safety. It was a fairly conventional dream-beach, a pleasant sunset illuminating golden sands, palm trees, and small breakers rolling in from the peaceful ocean. Paul felt a familiar urge to stay in this place of safety, but it was not his destination. It was the antechamber to something far worse.

Now that he was in a hypnotic trance, Doctor Blume guided him toward Liz, trapped in her labyrinth of mirrors. His point of view shifted as he left the pleasant beach behind, sped over the dark waters. The doctor's voice grew fainter as he neared the place of torment. Liz's mental prison rose ahead of him, a point of garish brightness amid the wider gloom. Every time Paul ventured into this world, he found it slightly changed, indicating the unstable and fluctuating state of dead girl's mind.

Sometimes, he found things were worse, the images in the mirrors surreal in their monstrousness. Other times, though, there was a slight improvement. Tonight, as he closed in on the cowering, gray-clad figure, he saw her image in dozens of shiny surfaces. Liz was an ugly creature here, sometimes broken and crippled, sometimes riddled with disease, her flesh covered with weeping sores. But, Paul realized, much of this suggested she was the victim, not the villain. He could see no caricatures of Liz the killer, so common in her earlier nightmares.

"Liz?" Paul said gently, walking along the too-bright passageway toward her. "Liz, I'm here to set you free."

He had made the offer many times, offered her his hand, wanted to lead her away from the mirror-maze and back to his place of comfort and solace. As he got closer, he heard Liz sobbing quietly. He sometimes forgot that, for all her power, she had died as a sixteen-year-old girl after a life of neglect and abuse.

"Liz?"

He hunkered down and reached out to touch her shoulder. She was thin, bony even, a malnourished teenager. Food, he knew, had been rationed throughout her childhood. So had parental affection, judging by the little he had gleaned from occasional mental contact. The one person to show her what appeared to be love had, in fact, used her, left her pregnant, ultimately sent her down the route that led to Rookwood, and Palmer.

"Liz, let's go," he said. "Let's get you out of here."

She looked up. Her face was not truly human, more like that of a mannequin, a blank expanse of colorless flesh with rudimentary lips and nose. Only the eyes seemed truly alive, great dark pools leaking tears down dead cheeks. Paul felt himself drawn to those eyes, and with dream-logic started to fall forward. At the same time, she reached out and clutched at him, pressing her grotesque face against his.

"No!" he shouted. "No, not this way!"

The shining maze disappeared, and he was plummeting, flailing in a void. Around him memories flickered, erupted, faded like dying stars. They were partial and distorted, but amid them, he saw again the life of Annie Elizabeth Semple. It was a very ordinary life, he knew. And yet, seen from within, it was a whole universe of hope and suffering. It threatened to overwhelm him, absorb the essence of Paul Mahan, combine the soul of a living man with that of a dead girl.

"Let me go, Liz! This isn't the way!"

Paul sensed her desperation, the need for love always denied in life. She was avid in her desire to finally escape her terrible loneliness. He felt himself starting to lose mental coherence, coming apart at the seams. Fragments of his own life were bursting and fading amid the brighter, harsher memories of Liz.

"Trust me, Paul, this is how it should be."

Her words came from everywhere and nowhere, permeating every fiber of his being. He did not trust her, and she knew it. For all her desperation, he felt her slowly relinquish her grip on his mind. There was a momentary sense of overwhelming sadness, and then he was listening to a gentle, anxious voice counting down from one hundred. He opened his eyes to see Doctor Blume's anxious face, felt her hand on his forehead.

"Don't try to get up yet, Paul," she warned. "That was clearly traumatic."

"Ya think?" he croaked. "Wow, I feel like I'm going to have the mother of all hangovers after that."

"She was feeling unusually frisky, eh?" said Mike, rising from his chair in the corner.

Paul was still trying to regain his sense of self, wondering if parts of his remembered past had been destroyed in the onslaught. It seemed likely. But he could find no resentment in his heart for Liz.

"She did what anyone would do in those circumstances," he said wearily, swinging his legs off the couch, then holding still as dizziness struck. "She's desperate. At least I've got some new info, of a kind. Now I know how it feels."

Seeing the puzzlement on their faces, he tapped the side of his head.

"Now I know how it feels to be taken over, enslaved, whatever you want to call it. Palmer's victims must have gone through something like that, only it was after he killed them. I guess that might have made it easier for him to take their souls, the lack of a physical body to anchor them."

Seeing the doctor's expression, he reached out and gently touched the back of her hand. She flinched slightly, then smiled.

"And they didn't have a real expert to help them escape. Thank you, Judy."

Paul stood up carefully, tested his balance, then walked over to the window.

"No more fireworks?" he asked.

"All the craziness seems to have died down," Mike observed, holding up his phone. "Well, it's moved online, anyhow. No actual physical harm being done. Three dead at bonfire parties, dozens injured, everyone going crazy over the apparitions."

"George Brockley Whins?" Paul asked.

"Oh, God," Mike groaned. "The guy is trending. Big time. Now America knows who he is, the real Grade A internet loons can have their say."

The Englishman paused, laughed.

"Sorry, but you know what I mean."

Paul accepted a cup of water from Blume, who still looked anxious and unhappy. After swallowing a couple of mouthfuls, he nodded.

"Yeah, Whins has fired up the crazies. It seems like whatever anyone does to try and counter Palmer, he gets what he wants."

"I really think," said Blume, "that we should take it easy for a few days. Then see how it affects Ella. Liz has shown no sign of reaching out to her for some time now."

Paul rubbed his eyes and sighed. He was losing sleep, exhausting himself with these expeditions into Liz's version of damnation.

"Okay," he said. "Let's make it, say, twice a week from now on? I feel I might be making progress, really."

***

John Beynon steered his dilapidated Renault into a back alley. By day, he would be reluctant to park anywhere in such a neighborhood, let alone out of sight of the main street. But on a rainy night, at three in the morning, he doubted his car would be molested.

"And if it is, my dear, you can deal with it, I'm sure," he murmured.

A ripple of shadow in the back seat showed that his words had been heeded. Satisfied, Beynon got out and raised his umbrella. As he emerged from the relative shelter of the alley, raindrops began to spatter on the black fabric above his head. He paused, looked up and down the street. Nothing moved in the gloom. He went on, passing a run-down pub with a 'For Sale' sign, then some nondescript buildings, and finally reached the church.

Again, he paused, raising his umbrella to look up at the Victorian Gothic building. Staring at it, he decided it had never been beautiful, and it was far gone in decay now. The churchyard out front was overgrown, tombstones tumbled and smashed by vandals. A notice on the wrought-iron gate informed him that the building was condemned.

Appropriate, he thought. *A dying building, waiting for the coup de grace.*

The gate creaked alarmingly as he pushed it open. A padlock and chain lay just inside on the overgrown pathway, the chain neatly severed by bolt-cutters. Beynon walked up to the church entrance and saw the door was slightly ajar. Inside, a faint light flickered. He looked around and spotted two figures, spaced some distance apart, observing him through the fence around the churchyard.

The congregation is gathering.

He climbed the two cracked steps to the porch and pushed the door open. Instantly, the light inside went out. He furled his umbrella then put his hands up, as if in surrender.

"It's me," he said. "Beynon. You know me."

A flashlight beam stabbed out, played over his coat, dazzled him for a moment, then flicked off again. Luminous green and orange blotches swirled across his vision. He stepped forward a couple of paces, then stopped, letting his eyes adjust to the gloom. The dirty, half-glazed windows of the church admitted a dim light from the street. In it, he could make out at least a dozen people standing or sitting near the bare stone altar.

Behind him, the door creaked, and Beynon stepped aside quickly as another person entered, followed by more. The church soon felt, if not exactly full, then no longer abandoned. It was hard to make out much in the dim light, but Beynon could hear plenty. He heard wheezing, bursts of ferocious coughing, and someone—a young woman, it sounded like—muttering incessantly, broadcasting her inner monologue to indifferent bystanders.

Beynon could smell the others, too, even over the fragrance of the expensive cologne he had applied earlier. There was a pungent odor of urine that might, perhaps, have been present already in the disused building. There was also the smell of sweat, cheap cigarettes, and alcohol. Beynon was almost sure he could detect methylated spirits wafting from a bulky figure standing a little too close on his left.

This is a place of despair, he thought, his mind cool and detached. *A congregation of the lost, the failed, and the lonely. With a smattering of the angry and paranoid, no doubt.*

As if to confirm his judgment, a rough voice suddenly shouted, "Get on with it, then! We haven't got all friggin' night."

Beynon stifled a laugh as the words echoed under the ramshackle roof. As rituals went, this one lacked the style of Hollywood movie Satanism. But behind it was something far more authentic. A figure detached itself from the crowd and shambled up to the altar. In the near-darkness, Beynon could only see that it was a large, hefty individual. A moment later a gruff male voice with a strong Scottish accent confirmed his guess.

"We all know why we're here," said the nameless man. "I found this place, or he found me here, I dunno. I was out of my head that day, wasn't I?"

There was a ripple of laughter at that. Beynon did not join in. He was concentrating, waiting for the first hint of what was to come.

"So he told me to go and get some more people, so we could join him, and get out of this shitty life, and... you know... live forever, like. So I went out and told people and they laughed. Some of them. But some of them didn't... and then people came..."

The *ad hoc* preacher suddenly doubled over in a paroxysm of coughing. Beynon shuddered, imagining blood and perhaps some lung tissue spattering on the dusty stone floor. For a moment it seemed as if the Scot would collapse completely. But the man slowly drew himself upright again and continued his impromptu sermon.

"There's nothing in this world for us, nothing in this life!" he shouted. "That country out there, it's been taken from us, and our future, all our happiness... all stolen!"

Angry cries of agreement came from all around Beynon. For the sake of appearances, he, too, shouted and cursed as the Scotsman ranted on. And then, without warning, Beynon could feel it begin. A tingling sensation ran over his arms, legs, torso, as if dozens of tiny electric shocks were being inflicted on his skin.

Protection working as advertised, one hopes, he thought. *Thanks, Thibaut, wherever you are.*

A few moments later the Scotsman stopped his nihilistic diatribe. The gentle prickling of his skin continued, but now it was mixed with another sensation. The air in the church had been cold and dank. It suddenly became icy, and even in the faint light, Beynon could see his breath in front of his face.

"He's come!" declared the Scotsman, turning to face the altar. "He never lets us down!"

In the tall, pointed archway behind the altar, Beynon saw shadows start to roil and pulse. A cloud of blackness bulged out into the church, and the altar faded, as if concealed by smoke. The cold was piercing now, and Beynon heard a feminine whimper from somewhere close by. Nobody retreated, however. Nobody made for the exit.

How much despair and hatred and confusion, he wondered idly, *does it take to keep them here, facing this monstrosity, in the hope of some unimaginable deliverance?*

The shifting mass of darkness began to shrink, becoming a rough sphere, then forming into a recognizably human shape. Beynon instinctively took a step back, then forced himself to stand still. Nobody else had flinched at the appearance of Palmer, or rather, what the doctor had become.

The shape on the altar was, Beynon saw, at least eight feet tall, with broad shoulders and an impressive build. It was not the short, plump psychiatrist who had lived and died back in the mid-twentieth century, but Palmer's own idealized version of himself. Yet, even now, the featureless face atop the colossal body showed for a moment the gleam of two small, round lenses.

"I am your deliverer."

Beynon flinched, as did most of those around him. Palmer's words were almost deafening, seeming to come from all sides at once. Yet they did not echo at all, and after the words were spoken, he had the sudden sense they came from an infinite distance, despite the immediate presence of the Palmer entity.

"Deliver us!" shouted the Scotsman.

Others quickly took up the chant as the towering figure on the altar scanned the motley assemblage. The ragged chorus of desperate voices ended as Palmer spoke again.

"I will punish those who rejected you. I will punish the persecutors. The proud will be humbled, the powerful destroyed, the deceitful brought low."

Beynon's skin felt as if it were crawling with ferocious, biting insects. He wondered if his protection would prove adequate this time. He began to focus on an internal mantra, a kind of protective incantation against the dark deity on the altar.

"Who will join with me?"

This was the crunch moment. Beynon had never heard this question before. It represented an escalation on previous ceremonies. For a few seconds, nobody responded. Then the young woman who had spoken her thoughts in an obsessive monotone pushed forward, ran to the base of the altar and fell to her knees. The monstrous shadow began to descend, losing its man-like shape. Others joined the woman, some running, others shambling painfully, but all eager to be one with their new god.

Beynon forced himself to stay put, fighting an urge to simply flee the church. He knew what came next might provide vital information. As he watched, the Palmer entity flowed down and over the supplicants, and for a moment they vanished. Then Beynon saw them lifted, one by one, into the air.

The entity began to rotate, becoming a freeing vortex of air that carried a dozen or more people around, carrying them toward the center of the church. Those who had not volunteered fell back, and Beynon joined them, as they gazed up at the dark figures circling above. A cold wind sprang up, swirling dust and litter around Beynon's feet.

He waited tensely, expecting Palmer to harvest the pathetic souls who had willingly given themselves. But instead, one of the drifting bodies descended, gently, to land with a soft thump on the stone floor. Soon all of the volunteers were released and showing no apparent ill-effects. All got to their feet, stared up at the Palmer entity as it reformed at the altar.

"You may now go about your master's work."

The entity vanished without another word. The ones who had been possessed walked stiffly to the door and left. The others watched them go, then began to file out slowly. Beynon, heart racing, felt the tingling on his skin subside. He resolved to not go there again, feeling that he had learned as much as he could.

I was a little too close this time, he thought. *No protection is perfect.*

As he stepped outside the church, he felt the rain on his face. He was about to open his umbrella when a heavy hand fell on his shoulder. He was spun around and a meaty fist punched him in the mouth, sending him flying backward down the steps and onto the overgrown pathway. He tasted iron, blood from a split lip.

"Right," said the Scotsman, stepping down to stand over Beynon. "You and me, posh boy, we're going to have a conversation. Because there's no way you're one of us, not with your nice car, your fancy accent, and your good umbrella."

The man swung his foot back to aim a kick at Beynon's groin. But before he could follow through, a figure appeared at the man's side. It was slender, about six feet tall, its form that of a hooded and cloaked person who seemed to shimmer. The Scotsman, caught off balance, stumbled sideways, then lashed out. His hand passed through the newcomer. Beynon, getting to his feet, smiled painfully at the thought of the man's confusion.

"She's not so different from Palmer," he said. "But the Dark Lady happens to be on my side."

His assailant swore loudly and flung another punch. The paramental shimmered away, then darted with unnatural speed. The

Scotsman's head was covered by the dark hood. He began to yell in panic and his arms flailed wildly. Then, with a choking noise, he fell backwards. There was a sickening crack as the man's head connected with the edge of a church porch step.

"Oops," murmured Beynon, brushing down his coat and picking up his umbrella. "A nasty accident. But if these people will drink to excess..."

He turned to walk to the gate, his shrouded companion dogging his steps. In the distance, far above the city, a solitary rocket soared into the night. It exploded in a shower of red sparks that quickly faded.

"What ephemeral creatures we humans are," Beynon muttered to himself as he opened the gate. "But some of us do aspire to more."

CHAPTER 5

The following morning Paul awoke bleary-eyed from a dreamless sleep and checked his phone. It was six forty-two. He grew tense, as he always did, when he saw a message from Neve Cotter. But when he opened it he was glad to see Ella had had a quiet night. 'Whatever you're doing, keep doing it,' Neve urged.

Paul sent an optimistic reply, not including any detail to his latest dream-encounter. He wondered for a moment if he should talk to Neve face-to-face. He decided to put off suggesting a meeting. He felt washed-out, surrounded by potential threats. He checked the news to see just how much damage Palmer had done.

Three dead, now. Over a hundred injuries requiring hospital treatment.

Not surprisingly, news of the Bonfire Night chaos was bound up with George Brockley Whins. The politician was doing the rounds of the news networks, having apparently mastered the trick of needing no sleep. Paul mentioned this to Mike as he entered the kitchen. The Englishman looked up from the cooker, glanced at the television, where Whins was being interviewed. Paul was glad the sound had been turned down, but the subtitles made it clear that the MP was making the most of his time in the media spotlight.

"Members of Parliament often ramble on deep into the night," Mike said. "They all tend to get by with very little sleep."

"Lucky bastards," Paul grunted. "I see he's still banging the drum about a government cover-up. Some awkward questions are being asked. And your government is as slippery as mine when it comes to answering."

Paul sat down, poured himself some coffee.

"You don't think Whins could be right?" he asked Mike. "I mean, maybe there is some deep state stuff going on?"

Mike shook his head and flipped over a frying egg.

"I doubt it. Palmer's too weird, too far outside the wheelhouse of government. Whins is even implying that Palmer's original experiments might have been government-funded, that there's a cover-up. It's just a way of keeping the pot boiling, I daresay. I mean, if it was a Ministry of Defense project, or an attempt to create telepathic spies for MI6, why do it in an asylum? They would just have gotten some hapless soldiers to volunteer, the way they did with atom bomb tests and LSD trials. You want one fried egg or two?"

"Just the one," said Paul. "I'm going to be spending more time sitting on my ass tutoring. I'll go for a jog later to work off the flab."

Mike set a fried egg on toast in front of Paul and settled down to eat an enormous bacon sandwich. Knowing what the response would be, Paul resisted the temptation to say that cholesterol might kill his friend. They might both face a lethal threat from Palmer at any moment. Paul suspected it was only his link to Liz, Palmer's killer, that provided him with some kind of protection. How far this might extend to his friends was anybody's guess.

"Well," said Mike, wiping his mouth with a napkin, "that's me done. Primed to deliver wisdom to the young, whether they want it or not. Oh, bugger, is that thing going now?"

The TV set had flickered, the picture becoming a blur of fading pixels before the screen went black. Mike did not have time to pick up the remote before the set came back to life. Paul noticed the electric oven's timer had also reset itself and pointed it out. A burglar alarm started screeching somewhere in the street, then another.

"Power outage," said Paul.

"Yeah," said Mike, putting the remote down by Paul's elbow. "Could be. Not the way I'd bet if I were a betting man, though. See you later."

Paul finished his breakfast and went into the living room. He set up his laptop and began to try to earn an honest living.

***

On the Metro platform at Blaydon Avenue, Yasmin Khan contemplated death.

She had walked through drizzle to the station, leaving her shared home early, deliberately avoiding her housemates. The violent chaos of the previous night seemed to sum up her own situation. For days, she had felt despair and futility welling up inside her, the loneliness of being friendless in a new town, the apparently impossible burdens of her course.

I'm not good enough, she told herself for the millionth time. *I thought I was clever, thought I could succeed. I was wrong.*

Yasmin was barely aware of the other commuters around her. Her thoughts were turned inward. She was ruthlessly scrutinizing her weaknesses, judging herself, finding herself wanting in every conceivable way. She had come to Tynecastle University with a sheaf of good grades and full of nervous anticipation. She had expected it to be difficult, a challenge, but she had faced challenges before and succeeded.

I was wrong. It's too hard. I keep making mistakes, I don't understand the lecturers, I daren't ask questions in tutorials. I might as well be invisible.

Yasmin moved forward a small pace to the edge of the line of red tiles that ran parallel to the edge of the platform. She was still in the safe zone, the area where you were supposed to stand. It was such a short journey she was contemplating, just two more steps, and then she would be over. The whole universe seemed to shrink to the area of the platform, the rails, the roar of the oncoming train that would emerge from the tunnel and solve all her problems forever.

There's only one cure for this loneliness.

A high-pitched giggle from somewhere behind her shook Yasmin out of her bleak introspection. She looked around and saw a tiny girl, no more than four years old, struggling to furl a small pink umbrella. Her mother stood over the girl patiently, clearly resisting the urge to do the job herself. The girl's face, wonderfully expressive, went from amusement to mild irritation to intense concentration. After a few more moments, she won her small battle. Mother and daughter exchanged smiles, the girl triumphant, the mother proud.

Yasmin smiled, felt tears pooling, and blinked them away. She thought of her own little sister, feisty and determined, never a quitter. She thought of her mother, her father, her brothers, and her family beyond that. She was not truly alone, and never had been—she was merely far from home. Her mind told her that, even while her emotions kept hammering at her self-esteem. She looked down at the dull metal of the tracks again.

The station seemed to become colder, Yasmin's breath visible before her face. In the distance, she could hear the screech of the approaching train into the city. The voice in her head multiplied, became a chorus of voices urging her to jump.

Finish it now!

"No," she said quietly. "No."

In that moment hope triumphed over despair. The little girl with her pink umbrella, struggling but ultimately triumphant, had been an epiphany. Yasmin reminded herself of the praise lavished on her by her teachers, the high school principal, and the enormous pride her family felt in her. She smiled, looked up the tracks to the tunnel mouth, resolved to step onto the city-bound train and have a good day.

Yeah, there'll be challenges, she told herself. *But life's one big challenge. I can fold up my pink umbrella. I can do this.*

The light of the Metro train appeared, gleaming on the curved tunnel walls. Yasmin took a step back, away from the red line. Or she tried to, because she must have collided with someone close behind. Still smiling, she turned to apologize, her instinctive response to any such incident. But there was nobody there. The nearest people were the mother and daughter, now looking on in puzzlement some three yards away.

Yasmin's mind struggled to grasp the impossible fact that someone was impeding her, that she could not step away from the edge. Panic began to grow as the station filled with the roar and rattle of the train. And then an invisible hand pushed Yasmin, hard. Off balance, in total confusion, she cartwheeled her arms as she stumbled backward and into the void she had just rejected.

The last thing she heard was a little girl, screaming.

***

Paul was deep in the middle of someone else's essay crisis when his phone rang. He tried to alleviate the student's concerns and let the call go to voicemail. But he froze when he heard the smooth, slightly smug tone of John Beynon.

"Hello, Paul! Good news. Despite losing a copy of the volume in question in a rather unusual accident, I may have been able to source another. With luck I should have it in a few days—I've already sent a message to Mike. Please get in touch when you have the chance. Goodbye. And *nil desperandum.*"

Never despair, Paul thought automatically. *Latin motto of this town.*

He continued to try and help the student online and, eventually, got the job done. He felt a slight glow of satisfaction as he finished the last of his coffee, which had gone cold. Then the client calling herself CindyCross008 logged on, and immediately began asking him for help.

'What's up?' he typed.

'It's weird,' she replied. 'You know all this crazy stuff in the news? About Palmer and the firework displays? I was dreaming about that.'

Paul sat unmoving, fighting an impulse to simply log out straight away. If he did that, he might trigger a complaint, and he could not afford to lose any source of income. Eventually, another message flashed up in the chat box.

'Hello? You still there?'

'Yes,' he typed. 'I'm here. It's only natural to dream about stuff that's shocking or disturbing.'

There was another pause, and he hoped for a moment the student would move on to something relevant, something purely academic that he could help with.

'But there's something else,' CindyCross008 typed. 'In this dream, I was in that asylum. I was kept in a filthy room that had padded walls. And this little man with glasses was there, and he was doing experiments on me.'

'Cindy I can't talk about this it's not part of this tutors job,' he typed. 'Do you want to talk about your studies?'

Paul waited, feeling slightly embarrassed at the way his over-hasty reaction had wrecked his punctuation. Seconds passed, and then the reply came.

***

Nathaniel Farson was about to sign off the night shift three hours late when he got the assignment. His boss told him that nobody else was available, which had become a familiar mantra. And Farson had, after all, finished his report on the Tyne Bridge jumper, while the death of Declan Mooney was in limbo awaiting a coroner's inquest.

"You have a fairly light caseload at the moment, Nat," the superintendent had said, apparently without a hint of humor. "And we need to be seen thoroughly investigating these student suicides."

It took two hours for Farson's team to take statements from the driver, the witnesses on the platform, and the people in the front carriage of the train. All were traumatized. Every time he completed an interview, the detective felt ashamed that so little help would be offered to bystanders struggling to cope with this tragedy. Budget cuts to the force meant basic policing and precious little else.

After the station had been re-opened Farson decided to review the security camera footage. There were inconsistencies in the eyewitness evidence, as usual. People were not good at recalling events, even in the best circumstances. Most had not been looking at the crucial moment, though too many had seen the horrific aftermath. Counseling was offered as a matter of course.

But, even taking into account the inevitable confusion, Farson was sure there was something odd about the student's death. When he checked the tapes, he was proved right. He quickly obtained a digital copy of the crucial sequence. He decided to take a chance and break the rules.

Getting to be a habit, he thought, as he uploaded the video to his phone.

He took a toilet break and, sitting inside a cubicle, sent the video to someone who was certainly not authorized to view it. Then he texted Paul Mahan and Mike Bryson. He returned to headquarters, so sleep-deprived that he felt a weird sense of detachment from all around him. He knew he was on autopilot and should get some sleep as soon as possible before he made a bad error. But he had one more thing to do. Farson contacted the university, a sadly familiar ritual. He felt sure he knew which department Yasmin Khan had been studying in.

Computer science, he thought. *Every single one.*

Finally, Farson got to go home and get some sleep. He woke to find a message from Mike Bryson, proposing another meeting that evening. He agreed.

***

"Well, gentlemen, here it is," said Beynon.

Paul and Mike looked on in astonishment as the book dealer lifted a large, black garbage bag and dumped it on the living room coffee table. Seeing their expressions, Beynon laughed.

"Take a look," he said. "It's fascinating."

Tentatively, Mike unfastened the top of the bag and looked inside. Then he reached in and pulled out a bundle of what looked like light brown confetti. Paul suddenly grasped what he was seeing.

"Shredded books!" he exclaimed.

"Exactly," Beynon said. "Some of my own stock suffered the same fate as that of dear old Lance. And that included my only copy of Thibault de Castries' book."

Mike threw the handful of debris back into the bag.

"Is this some kind of joke?" he asked.

"Not at all," said Beynon. "Let me explain. Palmer clearly destroyed the books, my copy and those of Lance Percival, because they represented a threat. So it seems obvious that, if I simply bring another copy within our enemy's field of operation, he will attack again. Yes?"

"Yes, I suppose so," said Paul.

"Take a seat," added Mike. "I have a feeling this is going to be a long conversation. Tea or coffee?"

"Your instincts are correct," said Beynon brightly, seating himself on the sofa. "Tea, please. Milk, no sugar."

While they waited for Mike to return, Paul made slightly stilted conversation with Beynon. They discussed the attack on his stock of rare books, which the dealer admitted had cost him thousands of pounds.

"So how can we access de Castries' book?" Paul demanded. "Do we come to Durham and consult it there?"

Beynon shrugged.

"You could, of course—when I obtain the volume from a trusted source, I will keep it locked away in my safe. But there is another option. I've already had my fellow dealer—who wishes to remain anonymous— scan some of the pages of *Megapolisomancy*. He emailed me the pages, and I have them here."

Beynon reached inside his jacket and took out an e-reader. Paul, despite his mistrust of the man, was impressed. For all his slightly fuddy-duddy manner, Beynon was trying to out-think Palmer using modern methods. A couple of minutes later the three of them were scrolling through the first chapter of de Castries' bizarre book.

"His prose is fairly terrible," Mike observed. "But he had plenty of energy. If the guy had taken to fiction, he might have been another Sax Roehmer."

"Quite!" said Beynon. "Thrilling adventures with unlikely plots. But de Castries was quite serious about his theories, for all his overheated style."

Paul was slightly disappointed. De Castries, like many writers on occult matters, was a windbag. He devoted a lot of time to proclaiming his own genius and denouncing those who failed to acknowledge just how great his ideas were. But it seemed Beynon's description of the book had been accurate. De Castries had been fixated on the idea that large, modern cities were the ideal breeding ground for paramentals, which were somewhere between the traditional ideas of ghosts and demons.

"Okay, the guy was on to something," said Paul, leaning back and blinking. Reading off a screen after spending much of the day online was giving him eye strain. He blinked again, peered out the window at the November night. It was still raining, the British weather living up to its reputation for dreariness.

"You okay?" asked Mike.

"Yeah, just need to rest my eyes," Paul replied, standing up. "Getting a bit spacey, staring at screens all day."

As he walked over to the window, he saw glowing blotches in front of his eyes. Behind him, Mike and Beynon were chatting about the details of de Castries' theories. Outside, Paul thought he could see a thin, dark-clad figure by the streetlamp across the road. He wondered who would stand out in the rain.

"Somebody might be watching the house," he said, glancing back at the others.

But by the time Mike and Beynon had joined him, the watcher—if they had ever been there—had gone.

"Probably just one of the local kids," Mike opined. "Bit sad, hanging around alone out there when it's pelting down, but—"

The lights flickered, then went out. The streetlights were still on, Paul noticed.

"Maybe a fuse has blown?" he suggested.

But then he felt the temperature start to plummet. What's more, his laptop, which had been running its screen saver, was now displaying random fluorescent dots as if it were suffering some kind of digital stroke.

"I think we might have attracted some unwanted attention," Beynon said quietly.

There was a loud crash and plaster fell from the ceiling. In the near-darkness, Paul felt something brush against him, a cold presence not unlike a wintry gust of wind. The light from Beynon's e-reader started moving, and Paul realized it was being lifted into the air. Then, with terrifying speed, it shot toward him. He dodged, and the device smashed through the window.

"Jesus!" exclaimed Mike. "It's found us."

"You think?" Paul said, trying to stifle panic.

We're not ready for a showdown, he thought. *This is not fair, Palmer can't just come here and kill us.*

The coffee table shuddered and then rose, spilling cups with a clatter. The three men split up instinctively, realizing that they made an easy target if they stayed bunched together. Mike ducked behind the sofa just in time as the small table hurled itself against the wall and shattered into splintered fragments. The impact shook the room. Bits of plaster rained down on Paul as he made for the door to the hallway. He grabbed the handle, yanked it open, but then it was jerked out of his hand and the door slammed shut.

"We need to get outside!" he shouted.

Paul turned, thinking to hurl himself out of the window. He vaguely hoped that, in the small front garden, there would simply be fewer things for the invisible intruder to throw at him. But when he started to run for the window, a heavy armchair suddenly shot across the room and took him down, slamming him against the wall. Winded, he struggled in vain to shove the chair away.

"Metraton! Enitharmon! Tiriel!"

Paul heard Beynon shouting out what sounded like nonsense syllables. He wondered if the book dealer had gone crazy. But then, in the dim light spilling in from the street, he saw Beynon standing in the middle of the room, arms raised like a priest offering a blessing. Around him, barely visible, debris was circling, a whirlwind of smashed furniture, plaster dust, shattered crockery.

"Begone in the name of the Thousand Eyes! Desist in the name of the Wondrous Heart! Depart, I order you. Depart in the name of the Lost Septentrion! Depart!"

The icy vortex seemed to grow more intense as Beynon repeated his command over and over. But, just as Paul expected the man to be killed, perhaps torn limb from limb, the turmoil began to subside.

"Depart!" Beynon called out in a clear, resonant voice. "Leave this place, being of chaos!"

Suddenly the whirlwind subsided and the debris fell to the floor. Paul sensed something shoot across the room. With a crash, the glass that had remained in the window seemed to explode into tiny, glittering fragments. Then they heard a succession of car alarms start to bleat, one after another. Paul imagined an irate entity fleeing down the street, lashing out petulantly as it retreated.

The light flickered on, revealing just how badly wrecked the living room was.

"Jesus Christ," Mike said, emerging from behind the sofa. "I can't see my insurance company paying out for this."

"Was that Palmer?" demanded Paul, trying to keep his voice steady. "Did he attack just because we looked at an electronic version of the book?"

"That would make sense," said Beynon, offering him a hand. "Ups a daisy!"

Paul grasped Beynon's hand reluctantly and found that the man's skin was not, as he half-expected, cold and clammy, but warm and dry. Various parts of Paul's body protested as he stood up, and he hoped he was merely bruised. He hobbled a couple of paces and concluded he had a badly twisted ankle to go with bruised ribs and arms. Mike was all for calling an ambulance, but Paul dissuaded him.

"The less attention we get the better, I think."

Paul's notoriety had faded a little in the last few months, but thanks to *Great British Hauntings,* he was trending again. The three did some basic tidying up. Mike taped some old hardboard over the broken window, then offered the others whiskey before taking a drink himself.

"How did you do that?" Paul asked Beynon, carefully seating himself on the sofa. "Is that stuff from de Castries' book?"

"Not exactly," Beynon said. "I improvised a little, mixed up a few things I learned from my studies over the years. The secret is not so much in the specific formula, but using the words to focus one's will. Rather like a mantra. It's important not to be afraid, of course, because that undermines—"

A heavy banging on the front door interrupted Beynon. A moment later, Mike ushered Farson into the room. The detective stood looking at the mess, then focused on Beynon, raised a quizzical eyebrow.

"Quite a coincidence, Detective Sergeant!" exclaimed Beynon. "Many thanks to you and your team for so promptly informing me of the break-in at my storage unit."

"My pleasure," Farson said, in a neutral voice. Turning to Mike, he went on, "I heard about a disturbance here over the police radio, so I contacted my boss and persuaded them to let me handle this. You don't want uniforms stomping all over the place to no good purpose. And, by the way, what the hell just happened here?"

***

"Farson?"

Mia looked at the email, frowning. She and Laura had been interviewed by the detective after the chaos at Rookwood had left one of her team dead. But she could think of no reason for him to contact them now.

"Yep," said Laura, "he needs some help, apparently. And he doesn't trust his own people to do a proper job."

"I'm assuming it's some of your tech mojo he needs?"

In reply, Laura clicked on an attachment and a video clip began to play. It was monochrome, low-grade footage, but Mia still recognized a typical platform on the Tynecastle Metro and felt a sick sensation in her stomach. A dark-haired young woman was standing near the edge of the platform. Her face was turned away from the camera, but she looked to be staring down at the rails. A woman and a small child were a few yards away, and Mia smiled as the little girl battled with her tiny umbrella. The dark-haired girl looked back at the child before looking ahead again. She appeared to attempt to step back away from the rails but stopped and turned around. Then, without warning, she stumbled forcibly backward past the safety line, arms windmilling, as the lights of an oncoming train appeared in the corner of the screen.

Mercifully, Laura stopped the film at that point.

"Oh God," Laura said. "That was on the news this morning."

"What does he want?" Mia asked.

"He thinks there might be something on the tape," Laura explained, downloading the clip. "And I think he's right. Did you see the way she fell backward? No way was that deliberate."

"Not on her part," Mia agreed. "Let's get started."

It took less than an hour for Laura to clean up the grainy security camera footage. What had initially been a hint of shadow moving across the platform now had more clearly defined features. It was a man-like shape, but too large to be normal, standing behind the victim, apparently leaning over her at first.

"Like it's whispering in her ear," Mia breathed, as Laura advanced the film one frame at a time. "God, it's vile."

When the dark-haired woman turned around, the dark form seemed to retreat, shimmering then reforming. Then an arm shot out, shoving the victim in the chest, sending her reeling off balance.

"Not exactly subtle," murmured Laura. "That bastard. If he can't persuade them to kill themselves, he just takes them out."

A thought struck Mia, one she would rather not have had.

"Okay," she said, "we've established that it's Palmer. Farson must know it already, just wanted this as confirmation. He's trained to be thorough when it comes to evidence. But we haven't—we haven't followed through. Farson didn't ask us to do anything more, but..."

Laura looked up at her producer, realization dawning. She looked horrified but nodded in agreement.

"Yeah," she said. "We need to see how he does it, if we can. See how he enslaves them. If we're going to follow up the original episode, like the money men want, we'll need to go into this stuff. We could never show it on TV, but we need to see it."

Mia drew up a chair and sat beside Laura. The editor began to play the clip, one frame at a time. At a snail's pace, they watched Yasmin Khan's death approach. And then they observed what followed.

CHAPTER 6

Beynon left shortly after Farson arrived, promising to remain in touch.

"I hope," he said on leaving, "that we can work together to contain this Palmer monster. After all, we have such a broad range of expertise, quite possibly we're the only team that could hope to prevail."

After the book dealer left, Farson observed that he was a bit of a pretentious wanker. This broke the ice and the three adjourned to the kitchen to talk over the latest developments. Paul took a few moments to examine his bruises, and Farson helpfully concluded that 'probably nothing's broken'.

"Apart from my home," Mike put in. "Theory is that Palmer wants to stop us from finding out too much about him."

They discussed Beynon and de Castries' book, which Farson freely admitted was a bit beyond him. However, the detective did raise a point that had been worrying Paul.

"How did he manage to banish Palmer so quickly? Look at how little respect the doctor has had for mediums and priests in the past. They never stood a chance against him. Something seems off."

"Maybe," Mike said, "but from where I was standing—or rather, cowering—he seemed to do a damn good job. And can we afford to freeze him out if he is genuine? I hate to say it, but that pretentious wanker might be our most effective weapon."

Farson stared into his whiskey glass, snorted derisively.

"That shifty bugger Whins, plus Beynon, not to mention our friends in the media. Talking of which, I've got something to show you. I asked some friends of yours to help me, and they came up trumps."

Farson produced his phone and sent Mike the adjusted footage that Laura Blaine had provided a few hours earlier. Paul forced himself to watch the whole thing, feeling sick and ashamed, a voyeur at a tragedy. The room was silent as the video played through.

"Does it tell us anything new?" Mike said, quietly. "This is just—terrible."

"I know," Farson said, a catch in his voice. "But look at what happens just as—as the entity captures her."

Mike replayed the final, horrific sequence. A couple of people were rushing forward, too late to help, while others stood paralyzed from shock. A mother was clutching her little girl to her, a tiny umbrella laying forgotten on the tiled platform. Mike froze the image, then advanced it in steps. The dark presence stood almost motionless. A flickering shadow appeared from under the slowing train, and the Palmer entity seemed to flow like an amoeba, reaching out to grab and absorb the lesser form.

"We already knew this was how he did it," Paul pointed out.

"Keep watching," Farson urged. "See what happens to the entity next."

At first, Paul did not see it. Farson reached out and put a finger on the screen. Even after Laura Blaine had enhanced it, the low-grade video had almost disguised the crucial moment. A shadowy globule detached itself from the Palmer entity, drifted away, faded. It took only a fraction of a second.

"What was that?" Mike asked. "It's like the entity shed part of itself."

"Beats me," Farson admitted. "But it could be important."

Paul asked the obvious question.

"Are we going to share this with Beynon?"

There was a long silence.

"No," said Paul. "If we're voting, I vote no. Not yet, anyhow."

"I think it has to be unanimous," said Farson, looking at Mike.

"Yeah," Mike said. "I suppose this means we're the inner circle, and he's just an outside ally. That's about as far as we can go."

***

Neve Cotter insisted on her twelve-year-old daughter going to bed by ten PM. The usual upshot of this rule was that Ella went to bed at some point before midnight. Both knew this was not just childish resistance to parental routine, though there was always an element of that.

No, Neve thought, as she watched Ella doing her homework. *We're both afraid of what might happen when she's asleep.*

Paul Mahan had called earlier to explain that he and Doctor Blume were not going to tackle Liz that night. Previously, when Paul was not in contact with Liz, the long-dead girl had re-connected with Ella. The results had been nightmares and sleepless nights. The stigmata of partial possessions, marks of Palmer's restraints on Ella's wrists and ankles, had also reappeared.

But maybe we'll get lucky, Neve thought. *Perhaps Paul's efforts will have made things better, somehow.*

Ella looked up from her laptop.

"What's a chimera?" she asked.

Neve smiled. She knew full well it would take her daughter five seconds to look up an unfamiliar term on Wikipedia. Asking her mother for help was a way of reaching out, of making Neve feel better and starting a conversation.

"Ancient Greek mythical monster, I think," she said. "Part lion, part dragon, part something else. Possibly a goat."

Ella frowned, typed something into a search engine, then read from the screen.

"Well," she said finally. "That's just ridiculous. How would anybody think that was real?"

Neve sat down next to Ella at the dining room table and looked at the picture of the mythical beast. She tried to remember some of the books she had read as a girl. She had once loved myths and legends, tales of heroes. Now, they seemed very remote and harmless compared to a far stranger paranormal reality.

"Perhaps," she suggested, "ancient peoples invented monsters to represent things about themselves that they couldn't face directly? Feelings that had to be suppressed, ideas that were too frightening to admit. That might be why so many of them are mixtures that don't seem to make much sense. Because sometimes life doesn't make much sense, and it's scary."

Ella looked doubtful but gave a little nod. Then she closed the laptop and faced her mother directly.

"I'm ready to go to bed," she said solemnly. "But I would like you to leave the doors open, yours and mine. And the light on in the hallway."

Neve felt a rush of pride for her brave daughter and had to stop herself from trying to gather the girl up her arms. Instead, she nodded seriously and offered to make cocoa. Half an hour later, they were both ready for bed. After she pulled the covers over herself, Neve tried to relax, following the old routine she had taught Ella. Focusing on her own tired body was a way of banishing anxiety over what might happen during the night.

Go to sleep, toes, go to sleep, feet, go to sleep, legs...

The technique worked, because when Ella's screams woke Neve, it was from a dreamless sleep. Neve stumbled into her daughter's room and held her close as Ella sobbed and tried to get out some coherent words. At first, Neve assumed it had been another nightmare about Liz in her personal hell. But then Ella explained, haltingly, that she had seen something very different.

"It was the lady doctor who helps Paul," the child whispered. "Liz showed me. The lady's in that place with the bad man."

***

Judy Blume worked on case files until just before ten, then decided to try and get some sleep. Her boyfriend was away at a conference for a few days, and their apartment seemed over-large and too quiet without him. Once, she might have relished a few days alone at home, able to kick back and indulge herself. Now, all she could think of was the night outside, and the shadows within. Despite turning on all the lights, brightening every room, there were still patches of dimness. They seemed larger and more numerous every time she looked.

Frightened of the dark, she told herself as she brushed her teeth. *Some psychotherapist.*

Judy turned off her electric toothbrush, placed it in its recharger. The sudden absence of the loud, insect-like buzz let the silence rush in, or so it seemed. She turned on the radio in the kitchen, letting mindless DJ chatter and familiar classic rock banish the silence. It suddenly occurred to her that she could take the radio into her bedroom. It was just the sort of thing she would advise her insomniac patients to avoid. Free your place of sleep from all distractions, that was the standard approach.

This is no time for petty consistency, she told herself as she picked up the radio. *I need to hear human voices.*

Judy walked through the flat, turning off the lights one by one. She could not sleep in bright light, she was sure, but after a moment's hesitation, she left on the hall light, allowing a wedge of illumination to spill through her half-open bedroom door. The compromise seemed about right. She put the radio on her bedside cabinet and climbed into bed. Soon she was dozing, the sounds of the music channel proving surprisingly soothing.

"And now," announced the DJ, "a special number for Judy Blume, who's celebrating a really big occasion today."

She jerked upright, stared at the radio set. Its digital readout glowed balefully. The song playing was an old standard, a bit of inoffensive country-rock. Judy concluded that she had simply dozed off and dreamed the announcement. It was a classic rationalization. She tried to settle down again, wishing sleep would come.

The hall light flickered, then died. The radio, however, continued to play. The anodyne music changed in character, though, the beat slowing down, the singer's voice becoming harsher, mocking. She sat up, staring at the radio as it sneered at her.

Judy's in the dark, feeling so forlorn
Wonders if she's gonna make it through 'til dawn
Judy's in the dark, scared and all alone,
Wants to call for help, there's nobody on the phone...

Judy knocked the radio to the floor, where it continued to emit its mocking refrain. She snatched up her phone, woke it, only for the screen to erupt in a mass of random pixels. She got out of bed, ran barefoot to the hallway and the old landline phone. It buzzed and crackled but offered her no dial tone. She continued along to the front door, feeling her way now, determined to get outside and hammer on the door of her neighbor.

Her questing hands, stretched out ahead of her, failed to find her front door. For a mad moment, she thought she had gone the wrong way and was heading for the bathroom, but that made no sense. No, the hallstand with the phone had been on her right, so that meant the door was in front. But she had already walked a dozen or more paces, and that meant she had traversed the entire length of her hallway.

"Don't worry, Doctor Blume, you're in safe hands."

The voice came from all around her. It was a man's voice, cold and refined, somewhat high-pitched.

"Who is that?" she shouted, struggling to quell her panic. "What do you want?"

"You know that already."

The lights came on, but they were not the warm, friendly lights of her home. Judy blinked in the glare of old-fashioned incandescent bulbs blazing down from a high-ceilinged corridor. The walls were painted a sickly pale green. There were cold tiles under her feet. Ahead of her was a pair of swing doors with small, round windows. A sign above them read East Wing.

"No!"

She spun around to flee in the opposite direction, found herself facing a group of people in green, old-style surgical gowns. Their faces were masked, their hands gloved. The figure in the lead was shorter than the rest. Over the top of his mask, he regarded her with cold gray eyes behind quaint, round-lensed spectacles. Judy retreated, shaking her head, desperate to deny what she was seeing, but unable to banish the sight. Nor could she ignore the distant cries of pain and fury echoing along the stark corridors, and the powerful smell of disinfectant.

"Welcome to Rookwood Psychiatric Hospital, Judy," said Miles Rugeley Palmer. "I hope you will find your stay with us helpful."

"You're not real!" she shouted, colliding with the swing doors. "The asylum burned down! You're dead!"

The doctor pulled down his mask, revealing his pencil-thin mustache, his smug, purse-lipped mouth. He shook his head and started to walk toward her, leading his throng of anonymous followers.

"Tut, tut, we don't use terms like 'asylum', Judy! As a doctor, you should know better. This is the twentieth century, after all. And it's also the twenty-first, at the same time. Such are the wonders of my new approach to therapy! It can be both then and now."

The doors behind Judy suddenly swung back, and she felt strong hands grasp her by the arms. She screamed, struggled, kicked out, but her captors easily lifted her into a high, wheeled trolley and strapped her down.

"This is what you feared the most, isn't it?" said Palmer, standing over her. One of his assistants handed him a hypodermic that was half-full of clear, yellowish liquid. "It's not an uncommon weakness in our profession—the psychiatrist afraid they are going mad. Not that we should use that word, either."

"I'm not going insane, you're not real, this is a nightmare!" Judy shouted.

Even as she tried to deny the experience, however, the leather straps holding her down chafed her skin as she struggled. And, when Palmer stuck the needle into the side of her neck, the sting of it was all too real.

"Now," he said. "It's time to start your induction process."

They rolled her along the corridor into the East Wing, where the cries of the tormented grew louder, and the odor of disinfectant no longer hid the smell of sweat and excrement. The trolley crashed through another set of swing doors and she saw bulky, old-fashioned equipment lining one corner of the room.

"This," said Palmer, rubbing his hands in anticipation. "This is where we helped our patients discover their psychic abilities. Now it's the place where we bring new recruits into the fold, so to speak."

Judy began to struggle again as a padded bar was inserted between her teeth, and cold steel electrodes placed against her temples.

"Why?" she shouted, her words garbled from the bar in her mouth. "Why are you doing this?"

"Because I can, of course," replied Palmer. "And because you seem to be helping someone who has caused us a bit of bother in the past. Not too much of a nuisance, Mr. Mahan and his friends. But one must be aware of potential troubles ahead, and without allies, he is no threat. So..."

Palmer nodded at someone out of sight behind Judy's head. A blinding light seemed to blot out the room, the onlookers, the machines. Then she was at one with the Palmer entity, utterly subsumed into the doctor's ego, her knowledge and memories plundered.

***

Mike Bryson found himself suddenly awake, sure there was another presence in the room. He felt a momentary panic, started to curl up into a ball under the duvet, anticipating another paranormal attack.

"Don't be alarmed, Michael. It's only me."

Mike flicked on the bedside light, and saw a small, thin, elderly man sitting on the chair where Mike had thrown his clothes a few hours earlier. Lance Percival was dressed in a tweed jacket, a slightly rumpled shirt, rather worn trousers, and a pair of old brown brogues.

"Percy?" he said.

"The very same," said the dead man. "I was going to say large as life, but... Anyway, I thought I'd say goodbye. You were a good friend to an old bore in his twilight years. Not your fault it ended rather grimly."

Mike swung his legs off the bed, staring at his old English literature tutor. He recalled Lance Percival's memorial service, the clumsy attempts to say suitable things to tearful relatives.

"How can you be here?" he asked. "I thought—Palmer..."

"Oh, him. Awful man, no moral values. Not surprised he got himself killed."

The old man grimaced, as if Mike had mentioned a rather rude party guest. Mike began to reach out in wonderment, wanting to see if he could touch a ghost's sleeve, whether the rough wool would feel real. But Percy wagged a warning finger.

"Hands off, young man! First rule of ghosts: don't poke them. Now, this is important. He got rid of me because he doesn't need me anymore, he knows everything I did. But there's more to it than that. It seems that Palmer has his limits."

Mike blinked as he tried to comprehend what the man was talking about.

"Limits?"

Percy looked up, past Mike's shoulder, and smiled.

"Ah, she's still waiting for me," he said placidly. "We had so little time together, you know, when you think of the big picture. I must go."

The room was suddenly lit by a startlingly bright, golden light. The radiance came from behind him, and Percy stood up, gazing into it, his expression beatific. Mike resisted the urge to turn around, feeling intuitively that it was not for him. Not for anyone living, in fact.

The light faded, leaving the room in near darkness once more. Mike turned and stood up, walking over to the blank wall. He ran a hand over it, as if this might reveal some kind of mystical portal. Then he turned on the light and went back to sit on his bed, rummaged for pen and paper. Mike tried to write an account of what he assumed had been a dream.

"What's going on?"

Paul was standing in the doorway, disheveled, bleary-eyed. Mike tried to explain, struggling to recall what his old friend had said.

"Why would Palmer let him go?" Paul said, puzzled.

He sat down by the bed, rubbing his eyes.

"Palmer's ego needs subjects, slaves, whatever," he went on. "Why would he discard one? Especially a clever, knowledgeable individual like Percy?"

Mike pondered for a moment.

"One in, one out," he said. "Maybe that's how it works. And Percy had said Palmer didn't need him anymore, that the entity now knew everything he did."

Paul stared at the Englishman, remembering the footage of the death of Yasmin Khan. It had never occurred to him before, but perhaps there was a limit to how many individuals the Palmer entity could capture and control. Perhaps that limit had been reached.

"So, Palmer must be taking over very specific minds, targeting particular people," said Mike. "And then ridding himself of people who are no longer useful. Seems like an insult to poor old Percy, but I suppose it's good news, in a way."

They talked a while longer, agreed to offer Farson the new information, then both parted to get some shuteye. But just as Paul was going back to his room, Mike's phone rang. It was Neve Cotter, talking about a new kind of nightmare.

***

Doctor Blume's neighbors had contacted the police about shouting and screaming. The door had been broken open by an officer who had found the doctor laying in her hallway. The medical examiner explained that the cause of death was unknown, but suggested it was possibly caused by a heart condition.

"Undiagnosed condition, if that's the case," he added. "There's no sign of her taking any medication. But they do say we doctors make the worst patients."

The ME paused, and Farson waited for him to continue.

"Okay," the examiner said. "I know you do the weird ones. There are some anomalies. The marks on her wrists and ankles and the sides of her head are a little odd, I'll admit. It's as if she had been restrained shortly before death, but the neighbors are emphatic they only heard her voice. We'll know more after the autopsy of course, but I can tell you now, the coroner will ask some tricky questions."

Farson watched as the body was borne away, then looked around the apartment. In Judy Blume's bedroom, a phone and a radio lay on the floor. Otherwise, there were no obvious signs of violence, no hint of intrusion. But he felt sure the killing was linked to the student suicides, and possibly to another death.

"Any update on that down-and-out?" he asked the ME as they left the building.

"Pretty much what you'd expect," replied the examiner. "Belly full of cheap cider, went to sleep in an abandoned building, fell over, and cracked his skull. Might have been saved if somebody had noticed him lying there and called 999. But they didn't, so he died. Why do you ask?"

Farson shrugged.

"It was a wild night," he said. "And I've heard a few things about that area, that church specifically."

The examiner looked appraisingly at the detective, then said his goodbyes and left. Farson drove back to HQ through the cold autumn night. He had another report to write, more relatives to contact, and more information to impart discreetly to his unofficial associates.

But first, he thought, *a quick look at that deconsecrated church.*

When he pulled up near St. Jude's church, he sent a quick text message to Mike Bryson, emphasizing that he should not be called. He had no reason to suppose anyone was listening in. But he had become wary given the increased attention on Rookwood and its aftermath.

"Loose lips sink ships," he muttered to himself. "God, I need more sleep."

Farson got out of the car and flinched as a gust of wind blew rain into his face. The church, a blocky Victorian building of no obvious architectural merit, was just visible in the streetlights. The scene of the Scotsman's death was not taped off. No forensic work had been done. Budgets were tight, and it was assumed that any vagrant found dead had expired from natural causes.

The detective paused at the gate, looked around. He had the distinct impression of being watched and knew the homeless tended to congregate in this area. But nobody was in sight. The rain was getting heavier. He decided to look inside and then bug out. The door was not locked, a sign the church authorities had pretty much given up on the building.

Probably want it to become too decrepit to save, he thought. *A way of outflanking the 'preserve every old building' brigade.*

He took out his flashlight, shone it around inside before entering. There was, again, no sign of movement. He shut the door behind him and checked out the interior. In one corner, there were some empty bottles, cigarette butts, used condoms, used syringes. There was also the acrid smell of urine.

Familiar so far, he thought, wrinkling his nose. *The people who've been here are the people you'd expect to sleep down here.*

Farson was about to open the door to leave when he heard a slight sound behind him. His torch beam probed the murk but found nothing. He thought it might be a rat, recalled that nobody was ever more than about ten yards away from one. But then the sound came again, and it was not a rodent's squeak. It was a human voice, whimpering.

A kid, maybe.

Farson advanced toward the altar, half convinced the noise had come from there.

"Hello?" he called. "Anyone there? Come out, please. Show yourself. You're not in any trouble, I promise you."

The whimpering was slightly louder this time, prolonged. Behind the altar, in the gloom under a great pointed arch, a pale face appeared. It was a teenager, a boy it seemed. He was looking at Farson, eyes great pools of blackness from which tears coursed down a thin face.

"Hello?" the detective said, more gently. "You okay, son?"

"No!" bleated the youth and flung back his head.

Farson felt himself grow colder. A dark line circled the youth's neck, a mark Farson knew must have been made by a cord or wire of some kind. He realized suddenly that, up to this moment, he had kept his knowledge of the paranormal in a special compartment, separate from his workaday self and its sensible attitudes. Now, the barrier had come down, and he had to truly believe in things he had once thought impossible.

Like ghosts.

"What's your name, son? I'm Nathaniel. Friends call me Nat."

The youth sniffled.

"Carl," he said tearfully. "I'm Carl. I was with them all, and then they just pushed me out. They didn't want me anymore."

"Carl," said Farson, then suddenly realized he could not talk a dead boy down, had no convenient words of comfort. "Carl, what does Palmer want? What's he trying to do?"

The pale face seemed to collapse in self-pity and despair, then vanished. A faint, plaintive voice echoed for a moment in the dead church.

"I want my mum!"

Farson walked out into the night, shutting the door carefully behind him, somehow feeling a need to be tidy, to seal things off. Back inside his car, he sat in silence for a while, hearing rain spatter on the windshield, drum on the roof. Then he took out a spare notebook, one he had often used for unofficial purposes, and began to write.

CHAPTER 7

"After the disturbing events on the night of November the Fifth," said the announcer, "now come reports, and even phone camera videos, of what people say are ghosts. This clip was taken near the center of Tynecastle..."

Paul and Mike watched the report along with Neve Cotter, who had called first thing in the morning after dropping Ella off at school. Between them, they had tried to make sense of recent events. It was obvious that Mike's vision of Percy had been part of a wider trend. But the killing of Doctor Blume had left them all nonplussed.

"And scared," Mike added. "If Palmer is picking off people close to Paul, for instance, that means we both have a big target on our backs."

Neve did not reply, and Mike swore under his breath.

"I'm sorry," he said, "I engaged mouth before switching on brain, there. But the attack last night rattled me, I don't mind saying."

Neve smiled, a weary smile, but one that Paul felt was sincere. He had often wondered if Neve and Mike might get together. But he also felt, outside a Hollywood movie, romance when under immediate paranormal threat was not a sensible idea.

"Palmer was always afraid of Liz," Paul pointed out. "I think that's a point to focus on. The closer any of us are to her, the more likely he is to back off. And then there's his ultimate goal, which we know nothing about. Except that he craves fame, status, power."

"True," said Mike. "But, being dead, he's not in a position to be rich and famous in the normal sense. That's the kicker."

"You think he wants to reincarnate himself, something like that?" Paul asked, frowning. "Surely that would just make him vulnerable—he'd be a regular guy who could be thrown in jail. He's more powerful in his post-mortem form as this gestalt monster."

They fell silent. Neve looked out at the pitch-blackness beyond the kitchen window, and sighed.

"Winter's coming," she said softly. "It's so bleak. Ella should be looking forward to Christmas, chattering about presents. Instead, she talks about Hell. About a girl in Hell."

She looked over the kitchen table at Paul. Her gaze was direct, appraising.

"I used to think you were rather weak," she said. "I know that's not fair, because you didn't ask for any of this. It just happened, to all of us. That's why I want to do more, play a bigger role in the fight. Please, just find me something I can do."

Mike cleared his throat.

"You could leave town," he pointed out. "I mean, so could we for that matter."

Neve waved a slender hand, shook her head, her long, auburn hair rustling audibly above the pattering of the rain.

"There's no guarantee Palmer won't come after us, for a start," she said simply. "And his ultimate ambition must extend beyond one provincial English city. So running just postpones the showdown, doesn't it? Not to mention the practical, real-world problem of money. Moving is expensive, even for someone who can work from home."

Paul had a sudden brainwave, and almost laughed at how unimaginative he had been.

"Computers!" he exclaimed. "You design websites, right? That means you must have some pretty good computer skills. You can keep us straight on why Palmer might want to—to harvest the minds of computer experts."

Neve shrugged.

"Yeah, I suppose so" she admitted. "But I'm nowhere near as good as these poor students who've been dying lately. They were all at the cutting edge of hardware, coding, artificial intelligence—all the cool stuff."

They talked some more, Neve admitting that any knowledge of information tech, even her limited amount, was probably better than two guys with doctorates in the humanities.

"Ouch," said Mike, "but point taken."

The discussion moved on to their supposed allies against Palmer. Neve was skeptical about both George Brockley Whins and John Beynon. Apart from an instinctive mistrust of all politicians, she felt Whins had proved himself to be an unusually slippery specimen.

"As for this book dealer," she said, "he sounds creepy as hell. And isn't it very convenient that he finds a second copy of an immensely rare book in such a short time? Almost as if he's working from some timetable of his own, and you guys are just caught up in his plans."

Paul had to agree, though Mike seemed more inclined to give Beynon the benefit of the doubt. Paul reminded him that he had brought Max Rodria to Rookwood, and that brainwave had simply added the paranormal researcher to Palmer's collective.

"I'm sure you meant well," added Neve, seeing Mike's discomfort. "And I think we've all made mistakes. When things are this weird, nobody can instantly figure out the right thing to do."

"True enough," said Mike, placated. "We're all amateurs at this. Hell, how could there be any professionals?"

One of the things Paul liked about his English colleague was the way he never held a grudge, never stayed angry for long. The downside was that it made him trusting, optimistic.

But maybe we need someone with a positive attitude, Paul thought. *God knows, I have enough doubts for the whole team.*

"What about these ghosts people are seeing?" Neve asked, bringing Paul back from his short reverie. "I mean, even accounting for media exaggeration, it seems people are seeing the recently dead. They appear, they fade, poof! Why?"

Mike explained the idea that Palmer's power was limited, and that he could only control so many lesser individuals at a time. Neve nodded and came up with a surprising analogy.

"Atomic nuclei," she said. "Heavy atoms, like uranium and plutonium, are just over the upper limit of stability. That's what makes them dangerous. They shed energy, lose particles and turn into lead, which is a stable element. Perhaps a similar principle applies to the Palmer entity—add enough new souls to it, and it will fly apart."

"How do you know all this stuff?" Mike marveled.

Neve looked at him and laughed.

"It's basic science, Mike," she pointed out. "Also, I have a very inquisitive daughter, and I need to answer her questions on just about everything. I can point you to some YouTube videos if you like. The point is, the entity might disintegrate."

"Or explode," put in Paul. "Which would be a nice way to get rid of the old bastard."

Neve frowned at that.

"It's probably a bad analogy," she admitted. "We're talking about disparate individuals, after all. Some more powerful than others, but all under Palmer's control, harnessed to his massive ego. I can't see how you would overload that system. Ultimately, he decides which of the dead to harvest, and which to ignore."

The others agreed.

"All we can be sure of is that he needs more expertise on our digital world," said Paul. "That's something he never had much grasp of before I went and liberated him—like an idiot."

There was a moment's embarrassed silence, then Mike spoke.

"You did what you thought was right, mate, and it was bloody brave. Plus, that car was fully insured."

***

"Nice place you have here," said Whins, looking around the bookshop.

"I think we both know it's a rather grubby place," replied Beynon, with a smile. "But it suffices. And sometimes, it is advantageous to live in obscurity."

Whins felt a rush of contempt for anyone who would choose to live without fame or money. He had agreed to meet Beynon after discreet online exchanges over the past couple of months. Beynon had provided him with useful background on Rookwood, preparation for the day that was bound to come. Now that the day had arrived, however, Whins wondered how much use the book dealer could be in the future.

"Books, eh?" he said, as he followed the older man through the aisles between bookshelves. "Not a great reader, myself. Official reports, the papers, of course, briefings—that sort of thing."

"Regrettable," said Beynon over his shoulder. "There is so much of value to be found in books. But I suppose as things move onto the internet there will be less demand for reading matter. Attention spans grow shorter, minds grow shallower. It's just up here."

Grunting with the exertion, Whins followed Beynon up a narrow staircase to the dealer's cramped flat. Here, again, were stacks of books, most of them ancient and dusty. To Whins, they were a waste of space, and his doubts about the other man returned. The politician had already got his fair share of publicity. Some newspapers were calling for him to be taken back into government, given special responsibility for tackling the violence and chaos in Tynecastle.

"Tea?" asked Beynon, gesturing at a bead curtain that presumably led to some sort of kitchen.

"No, thank you," the MP replied, wrinkling his nose at the musty odor. "I am in a bit of a hurry—busy schedule."

"Of course!" Beynon exclaimed, gesturing at a saggy armchair. "Please take a seat."

Whins sat down carefully, wondering how much dust would mar his Savile Row suit. He had almost decided to cut ties with Beynon when the dealer surprised him with a new gambit.

"What is the point of power?"

Whins blinked, surprised by the straightforwardness of the question. He automatically went into interview mode, a time-honored tactic used to buy time.

"One only seeks power," he said, smiling, "in order to serve one's country. Public service is the highest of ambitions. I think it was Churchill who said..."

"Nonsense!" exclaimed Beynon, making an impatient gesture. "You're not on television now, George. You want power because you like power. In fact, you can't bear the thought of not getting it. It's a drug, an addiction."

Whins started to protest, but the book dealer cut him off again.

"Don't waste time denying it! Politicians vary a lot in character, but most want power and the status it brings. It's not enough to be merely rich or famous. There must be that frisson of power, of deciding the fates of others. Isn't that true, George?"

Whins again tried to deny what sounded very much like an accusation, but suddenly the dealer walked over to him, bent down, and looked him in the eyes. Whins flinched, glanced away. He normally had no problem facing a direct stare. But there was something about Beynon that made him uneasy, unsure of his ground.

"Now we've settled that," Beynon said, standing upright again, "let's consider how one might attain power. Or rather, how the two of us might."

"I'm obviously very grateful for your help with regard to the Palmer situation," Whins began, now even more determined to sever all links with this strange, disturbing man. "But I feel the time has come to... to... for us to go our separate ways, I mean... because..."

Whins found himself struggling to speak, as Beynon looked down at him, a smug smile on the dealer's face. The room seemed to fade as Beynon raised a finger and began to talk in a low, compelling voice. His words were fascinating, perfectly chosen, washing over Whins like a warm spring of rhetoric. Yet, when Beynon stopped, Whins could not remember anything that had been said to him.

"You see my point?" Beynon said brightly, lowering his hand. "We must work together."

"Yes, yes, of course," replied Whins, still slightly dazed. "We must work as a team, for the benefit of all."

Beynon smiled wolfishly at that, exposing a mouthful of startlingly big, yellow teeth. Whins sensed movement nearby, twisted around in his chair, but saw nothing in the poorly lit room. The bead curtain moved then, as if in a slight breeze.

"An old building," Beynon said, "very drafty, I'm afraid. Now, let us see how we can best go about thwarting the ambitions of that old monster, Palmer."

***

"Bloody hell," said Farson, gulping down the final dregs of a cup of cold coffee.

On the desk in his home office, he had spread out a collection of old, dog-eared documents recovered from police files. The information had not been digitized, and probably never would be. It consisted of reports dating back to the Fifties, all of which had been filed and forgotten. Farson had gone through filing cabinets in the cellar, looking for any cases that were out of the ordinary.

He had found little that was new about Rookwood or Palmer. Most of the information about the asylum and its boss was now in the public domain, thanks to the efforts of Max Rodria, Mia Callan, and others. But the same was not true of John Beynon, who appeared in the files several times. In each case, the dealer had been named as an associate of someone who died in odd circumstances.

"A rival book dealer," Farson mused. "And a private detective looking into a disappearance. Okay, that's intriguing stuff, but nothing very solid."

He leaned back, his chair creaking. His wife was at work, not due back until late, otherwise he would have called her in, discussed his suspicions. She was an excellent sounding board, always willing to offer a fresh perspective. Sometimes, she saw connections Farson missed in these old, cold cases—details that seemed irrelevant.

"Details," he sighed. "So many."

He flipped through the report of a long-dead detective, sighed again, and was about to put it back into its faded cardboard folder when he stopped. There was something, something obvious that he had missed it. He ran a finger down the thin sheet of carbon-copy paper.

"John Beynon, a man of about fifty," he read. "About fifty."

He checked the date on the report.

"1974. Well, that's bollocks. He doesn't look much older than sixty now. So, whoever typed this up from handwritten notes goofed. At a stretch he might have looked thirtyish back then, I suppose, but..."

He flipped open another file and found that, in 1988, an officer had described Beynon as middle-aged. But it was the third report that provided the key revelation. Dated 1967, it described Beynon as a man of about forty. Farson had a brief idea that the reports were describing two different people, perhaps father and son.

"Okay," he said, turning to his computer again, "let's see if there's any record of a Mrs. Beynon giving birth to a little bouncing Beynon at some point."

Another half hour had turned up no evidence of a John Beynon senior or a mother for the current man. Farson, however, resisted the other possible interpretation of these facts, or rather the lack of them.

"It's bonkers," he muttered. "Nobody ages that slowly. It's impossible."

***

The next few days passed without major incident, as if Palmer had decided to lay low for a while. The online clamor continued thanks to Mia Callan's film, but there were no more unusual deaths. Brockley Whins continued to seek publicity by demanding answers from a government which, it seemed, had none. Britain's long-drawn-out political paralysis continued as before, where contenders for power bickered to little real effect.

Meanwhile, Farson continued his investigations, and kept Paul and Mike up to speed. He alerted them to the anomalies about Beynon's age. One possible answer, they agreed, was that he had tapped some source of paranormal power to extend his lifespan. It was, as Paul said, just 'another good reason not to trust the bastard.'

It was at night that the biggest problems arose. Ella Cotter's nightmares returned and, without Blume, Paul was unable to seek out Liz and deflect her attention. However, Paul decided to try a different approach. He reasoned that Liz was constantly reaching out to the girl, trying to clutch at her as a drowning person might grab at a good swimmer. They met with Neve at her place, while Ella was staying overnight with her grandmother. Having a sleepover, Neve explained, seemed to calm the girl somewhat and let her sleep more deeply.

"But," Neve added, "it seems to wear off pretty quickly."

"Maybe," Paul said tentatively to Neve, "me simply being close to Ella might let me contact Liz. It has in the past."

"And it caused problems," Neve shot back, instantly on the defensive. "Liz can be very destructive."

There was an awkward silence, which Mike broke.

"You said it yourself, Neve, none of us asked for this," he pointed out. "We're all improvising, guessing, doing our best. Let's try Paul's idea. Without Blume it's that, or just, well, pray."

Neve looked down into her coffee cup, coppery hair gleaming. Paul wondered if she was close to her breaking point, for all her apparent confidence. She had been through the wringer, he knew, before she had even moved to Rookwood. The old asylum had left its mark on mother and daughter. Both had acquired the tired, slightly wild look of the long-term insomniac.

"All right," said Neve, finally meeting Paul's eye. "I do appreciate how hard you've tried to help, and we'll give your idea a go. If it doesn't work, I suppose I can fall back on sleeping pills of some kind—though how I'll explain it to our doctor..."

Neve's phone vibrated, then trilled urgently. She fished it out of her coat and, frowning, took the call. Paul saw her expression change from concern to alarm as she gabbled out questions.

"When did this start, mum? What's she like now? I mean... you didn't call anyone? No, no don't, wait till I get there. Just wait, mum!"

Paul was already putting his jacket on, while Mike gathered up his keys from the bowl on the hall table. Neve rapped out a few words of explanation, but it was already clear that Ella was in trouble. As they piled into Mike's car, Neve called her mother back, demanding more details, but became increasingly agitated and seemingly unable to take in what she was being told. Paul felt Neve was close to actual panic, but eventually Neve started speaking more calmly.

"Some friends are bringing me over," she said, "I'll be there in a few minutes. Yes, somebody with me can help, mum."

Oh God, Paul thought. *I hope she's right.*

***

The anonymous tip-off came at the start of Farson's night shift. He might have ignored it, just another one of dozens of claims from supposed informants that came in every week. But when the duty sergeant mentioned the location, the detective sat up and asked for more information.

"Listen for yourself," said the sergeant. "It's on the system. But it just sounds like another nutcase to me. We've got a prize crop this month."

Farson had to agree. Normally, most anonymous tips were petty and motivated by spite. A neighbor might call to get someone in, claiming they were dealing drugs, when, in fact, noise was the issue. Farson had investigated one case where someone had anonymously claimed the woman next door was running a brothel. It turned out the neighbor's real complaint was that the woman's cats were doing unpleasant things to his prized rhubarb.

However, since the Palmer entity had manifested itself on Bonfire Night, the craziness level had increased. People were reporting ghosts, angels, demons, and monsters of all kinds. Even if the police had had the resources to probe every report, the paranormal did not count as criminal activity. Farson ignored most of them. But this latest one concerned a location he was interested in.

Farson brought the call up on his screen, played the audio clip. It began with a distinctive click that told him someone had used one of the city's small number of pay phone booths. The sound quality was poor, and he could not hear every word. The urgency of the voice came through, however.

"They're all getting together... St Jude... dunno what's going on... weird. Needs looking into..."

Farson played the recording through a couple of times. There was something about the voice that sounded familiar, but he could not place it. The accent was local, working class, male, but of indeterminate age. Farson noted in his online log that he was going to investigate, and signed out.

Ten minutes later he was pulling up a couple of streets away from the deconsecrated church of St Jude. He decided to approach more cautiously this time, arming himself with a taser. The night was dry, for a change, but a stiff wind was blowing leaves and other debris along the street.

Okay, let's check out the spooky church.

Farson pulled up the collar of his jacket against the biting wind as he walked along the cracked, weed-infested pavement. The whole area was typical of the neglected districts of British cities; formerly thriving business districts where every firm had failed. Boarded up stores and warehouses rose on all sides. A few of the streetlights had failed, leaving great patches of gloom. He rounded a corner and saw the spire of St Jude's blotting out the glow of the city's night sky. He paused, stayed close against a wall, waited for noises, signs of movement.

Nothing. Probably a hoax call. A wino, maybe.

Again, something nagged at the back of his mind, something about the voice on the phone. Then he saw it, a blur of movement in the overgrown churchyard. It was not the gathering the tip-off had mentioned, but it was activity. Farson knew the odds were they were winos or vagrants. It could even be teenagers braving the cold for a quick outdoor shag.

But it might be something else.

Farson reached into his coat pocket, clutched the taser. In the past, he had wished he could simply draw a firearm from the arsenal at headquarters when he faced an unspecified threat. But he also reasoned that, facing the paranormal, it was impossible to know what mode of defense might work, if any.

Such a cheering thought.

The detective was about ten yards from the fence around the churchyard. There was no sign of movement now. But then he heard a distinctive creak, and recognized it as the church door opening, or maybe closing. He picked up his pace and was soon in sight of the porch. The door was open. Farson entered the churchyard through the open gate, took out a small flashlight, but did not turn it on. He did not pause in the doorway, aware of the risk of being silhouetted against the sky-glow. He dodged to one side, paused, waited for a sound of movement.

"Hello, Detective Sergeant!"

The hearty welcome echoed from cold, stone walls. In that moment, something clicked in Farson's mind, and he understood why the voice on the poor-quality phone line had sounded so familiar.

"You should be in showbusiness, Mr. Beynon," he said, moving further away from the door. He shifted the flashlight to his left hand, took out the taser with his right. "You do a good proletarian accent."

Farson collided with something hard-edged and wooden, something that clattered. It was probably an old bench. Cursing under his breath, he decided to simply leave. But then the door swung shut with a resounding crash. Startled, Farson raised his flashlight and flicked it on. The beam picked out a thin figure in a long coat, smiling calmly. Beynon had been behind the door.

"What's this all about?" Farson asked, stepping forward. "Why the cloak-and-dagger stuff?"

Beynon raised a hand to block the flashlight beam, his face vanishing in shadow.

"I think you know why, Nathaniel," he said quietly. "You've been far too helpful to your friends. I had you down as a typically unimaginative policeman, all bound up by rules and procedures and preconceived notions. But it turns out you are dangerously open-minded. I've been planning things for a very long time, and I've no intention of letting any troublesome individuals put obstacles in my path."

Farson sensed movement somewhere off to his left, flicked his beam around, swept it over jumbled, broken furniture and drifts of assorted garbage. There was nobody else in sight. He turned back to Beynon, who had stepped closer, almost within touching distance.

"Keep back," Farson warned. "You've already committed an offense by luring me here on a false pretext."

"Oh no!" Beynon mocked, holding up his hands. "Don't take me in, officer, I'm a good lad really. I just fell into bad company. Quite a long time ago. Starting with my father, as it happens. His name was Thibaut de Castries—does that ring a bell?"

"Rubbish!" said the detective.

"Your voice betrays you," Beynon observed. "You begin to suspect that you're in way out of your depth."

Again, Farson sensed movement, but did not take his attention from the other man. He could not quite believe Beynon would try to attack a police officer, in part because he now thought of the book dealer as a well-preserved centenarian. He flicked his torch beam up to shine it directly in the man's face again.

"The forces of light are faltering, Nathaniel," Beynon said, his tone suddenly devoid of playfulness. "See how easily the darkness wins?"

The flashlight flickered and died. Farson shook it, struck it against the taser, but it was dead. He felt a hand touch his shoulder, and lunged with the taser. There was a flash of blue light in the gloom as he pushed the button. He also heard a satisfying croak of dismay from Beynon.

"Oh, that was unsporting," said the dealer. "I was going to try and recruit you to my cause, but I think that might prove too difficult. So, I'll bid you goodnight, officer."

The door opened and, before Farson could react, Beynon had slipped out into the night, moving with surprising speed and agility. Farson, anger rising, decided to arrest the man for wasting police time. It was a trivial offense, but it would allow an investigation to begin, a case file to be opened.

Another surprise came when Farson reached the doorway and saw Beynon standing by the churchyard gate, face in shadow. The detective paused, wondering if this was a new move in Beynon's puzzling game. Then he felt something brush against the back of his neck, something cold and dry. It might have been a moth, or a falling cobweb. But then it returned, a sensation like a myriad of insect legs marching over his head and shoulders.

"What the—?"

Farson spun around to see a shrouded figure standing close. It was not quite as tall as he, and it was slender, its form suggestive of a woman in a hooded robe. But even in the dim light, he could see it was not human. The 'robe' shimmered and blurred, its folds shifting uneasily, and the opening of the hood revealing nothing inside.

Farson retreated, jabbed out with his taser. This time the device contacted nothing solid, but instead, encountered slight resistance as he activated it. Sparks flew, but the faceless figure did not show any ill-effects. Instead, it reached out with dark arms and cupped shadowy hands around his face.

The church, the run-down street, the whole world seemed to recede to a vast distance. Farson tried to resist but was unable to move. The nightmare being drew his face closer, until it was inside the spectral hood. He saw profound blackness, but it was a living darkness that exulted in his defeat, flowed into his soul like a stream of icy lava, and began to tear his mind apart.

CHAPTER 8

They found Ella curled up on the sofa in her grandmother's living room, wrapped in a blanket, and clutching a cup of hot milk. The girl was looking at a nature documentary, the soothing voice of David Attenborough turned low. Paul remembered that, in happier times, Ella had loved natural history, and had been a keen observer of birds, insects, flowers, and the like.

"Hello," said Ella, her voice weak, as she tried to smile.

Neve took her mother into the kitchen to try and explain the situation while Mike and Paul chatted with the girl. As expected, she explained Liz had been 'reaching up' to her from the bad place where the long-dead girl dwelt. Paul asked tentatively if he could see Ella's arms. The girl reached out one hand, and the sleeve of her pink dressing gown fell away to show a red welt circling her wrist. He looked down and saw a similar red ring around the girl's ankle. She quickly pulled her bare foot back under the blanket.

Restraints, Paul thought, examining the mark. *Barbaric, old-school asylum methods. I can even see the mark of the buckle.*

He let go of Ella's hand, but the girl suddenly clutched at his fingers. Her strength surprised him. It was, he realized, born of desperation. Her eyes seemed huge, pupils dilated, as she peered up at him.

"Help me, Paul," she said quietly. "She wants to live, escape from the bad place with all the mirrors. Because she saved me once, she thinks I owe her my life. That's not true, is it?"

The girl looked from one man to the other as Paul and Mike struggled to find the right words. Neve reentered the room and Ella let go of Paul's hand.

"I've tried to explain to mum," Neve said. "She knew something was up, but she never expected something like this. That said, all the weird stuff that's been going on has convinced her that Rookwood—well, let's just say she's suspended her disbelief. And she won't object, she just doesn't want to get involved."

Paul looked past Neve and saw Ella's grandmother pouring herself a glass of wine.

Wish I could join her, he thought, hunkering down next to the couch. Mike went into the kitchen and started to talk in a low voice to Mrs. Cotter, closing the door behind him.

"Okay," said Paul. "I think we're connected, Ella, because of Liz. So if we both concentrate hard, like we did last time, I think we can get in touch with her. And then..."

He hesitated and looked up to Neve, who was hunched forward in her armchair. Paul chose his words carefully.

"If we work together, we can get her out of the bad place, and lift her up, help her move on. I think I've come close to helping her escape, lately. We just have to be positive, and brave, and not let anything that happens scare us. Okay?"

Ella nodded.

"That was quite a good pep talk, Paul," she said. "You're doing your best, I know. But I think we'll both be scared, won't we? It's only natural."

He had to smile at her commonsense approach and reminded himself that a bright twelve-year-old sometimes saw things more clearly than a so-called adult. He reached out both hands this time, and she once more clutched at his fingers. Paul closed his eyes, took a breath, and tried to focus. He could not hypnotize himself, but he knew the essence of suggestion was relaxation.

"Close your eyes, Ella. We'll go together."

Without vision, the small sounds around him became louder. He could hear Mike still talking to Ella's grandmother, his voice reassuring, no doubt stressing how competent Paul was, describing him as a real-life hero. He could also hear Neve Cotter's breathing, fast and shallow, a mother stressed to an almost unbearable degree by a stranger leading her child into a dangerous place. And he could hear something else, now, a restive whimpering that must be coming from Ella. The sound was faint, and somehow remote, as if coming from a vast distance.

An illusion, he thought. *Mind playing tricks again.*

Suddenly there was light, his inner eye opening to a vista of the purgatory Liz had inflicted upon herself. The vast labyrinth of grotesque, funhouse mirrors spread below. As in previous sessions with Doctor Blume, Paul descended toward the maze, and waited for Liz to become visible.

At first, he saw nothing but shining corridors, over-bright and crazily chaotic in their layout. Then he glimpsed a small figure, dressed in the familiar stained cotton robe of Rookwood Asylum. He got closer and felt something was wrong. The mirrors around him showed nothing, none of the distorted and vile images of Liz he had seen so often before. He scanned them as he drifted ever nearer, waiting to glimpse the sore-covered plague bearer, the murderous whore, the pious hypocrite. But none of the twisted variants of Liz appeared.

"Liz?" he said, turning to the huddled figure in the corner of the cell at the heart of the maze. "Liz, does this mean you've stopped condemning yourself? Because that means we can go now, leave this place."

The small figure moved. Paul suddenly realized it was too small, too thin, to be Liz. The girl had been malnourished and undersized for a teenager but had never looked this frail. He had already guessed the face he would see when Ella looked up at him.

"Hello Paul," she said. "She told me we could both escape from the nightmares, but then when I let her hug me close, she left me here."

Oh, Jesus Christ, he thought.

"Have you come to let me out?" the girl asked.

"Yeah," he replied, trying to convince himself as much as Ella. "We need to... to work together, help each other to..."

He stopped trying to improvise some optimistic scenario, seeing the girl's expression.

Around them the mirrors vanished, the labyrinth disappearing like the bad dream it was, until all that remained was Liz's padded cell at Rookwood. Paul felt sudden constrictions at his hands and feet. Chains rattled as he tried and failed to pull himself away from the wall.

"Paul," asked Ella. "How do we get out?"

Paul looked around him, trying to fight down the despair that threatened to overwhelm him. He also felt anger, rage at his own stupidity, and fury at Liz for stealing Ella's body, displacing her soul.

"Paul?" asked the child.

The walls flickered for a moment, and beyond them, Paul saw something. It was the merest flash of what might have been the living world, a sane, living place. And there was a familiar face, seen only for a fleeting instant.

***

"What the hell happened?" demanded Mike, rushing back into the room, followed by Mary Cotter.

Neve was already on the floor next to Paul, turning him over, checking his pulse. Ella was staring, wide-eyed. Her grandmother put protective arms around the girl, led her out of the living room.

"He just collapsed," Neve said. "Maybe fainted? I dunno, he said something I didn't hear. Oh God, look!"

She held up Paul's limp hand and Mike saw a red welt around his friend's wrist.

He's in that padded cell, he thought despairingly. *He's trapped in Liz's private hell.*

"He needs help," Mike said, taking out of his phone. "God knows what we'll tell the paramedics. Best just say he collapsed suddenly."

Just over an hour later, Mike and Neve were seated in a waiting room. Neve checked her phone every few minutes but there were no updates about Ella. Mary Cotter had at first reported that Ella had finally gotten off to sleep. Later, she reassured Neve that Ella was sleeping peacefully 'like a little angel'.

"So whatever Paul did, he seems to have saved her from Liz's influence," Neve said, putting her phone away. "It's some consolation. Perhaps all that's happened is he suffered some kind of shock, and he'll be back with us soon."

Neve trailed off as a white-coated young woman came up to them and introduced herself as the emergency trauma registrar. The doctor told them that Paul had indeed suffered some kind of 'shock to his system', but it was definitely not a heart attack or—so far as they could tell—any kind of brain embolism.

"We're going to conduct some more tests, including an MRI scan," she said, "hopefully they'll give us more to work on."

The doctor paused and seemed slightly embarrassed.

"You weren't—playing some kind of game?" the woman finally asked.

For a moment Mike was nonplussed. Then he saw Neve's expression and realized what the doctor was implying.

Bondage games, he thought. *The marks on the wrists and ankles.*

"No," Neve said firmly, while Mike was still groping for words. "There was nothing like that. He just collapsed without warning, he—he has been under a lot of pressure lately, isn't that right, Mike?"

"Yes, definitely," Mike replied enthusiastically.

The doctor's brow furrowed.

"You know, one of our nurses said she recognized your friend's name from somewhere. Has he been on some kind of reality TV show?"

Mike and Neve looked at one another.

"I think," Mike said slowly, "we might as well come clean about it all. This is not one of your typical cases."

"Were you on duty on November 5th?" Neve put in.

The doctor's eyes widened, then she seemed to understand. She sat down and, for the next half hour, they discussed the paranormal in the brightly lit waiting room. Around them, normal people waited for science to solve the problems of relatives and friends. Mike felt a sense of disconnect between the setting and the subject. But, as they explained what they thought had happened to Paul, the doctor seemed more receptive than they could have hoped.

"Take it from me," she said finally, "I saw and heard so many weird things on Bonfire Night, that I'm prepared to accept—well, that your friend Paul has something a bit beyond my expertise. But we'll keep trying to help him, regardless. At the moment, all we can do is keep him comfortable, monitor life signs, make sure he doesn't get dehydrated and so forth."

After more discussion, the doctor promised they would be contacted if Paul's situation changed. Neve, looking a little uncomfortable, decided to return home. Mike was left sitting on a hard, undersized chair, watching the first of the evening's crop of post-pub drunks being brought in. He smiled grimly, remembering his own younger days in Birmingham, and wondered how his idiotic younger self had avoided ending up in the casualty ward back then.

"He is our god! You'll all pay when he takes over, oh yes. But we'll be raised up, mate, you wait and see. Yeah, you can laugh at me, you fat bastard, but just you wait! Your day will come!"

A swearing, struggling man in a motley assortment of old clothes was half-dragged, half-carried past the doorway. Mike leaned over to watch the impromptu show. The troublemaker was an older homeless guy with long, iron-gray hair and a wildly unkempt beard. Blood coursed down one side of his face, soaking into the neck of the ancient turtleneck he wore under an overlarge coat. The vagrant's feet were wrapped in newspapers. The man's eyes stared, unblinking, at Mike for a moment.

"Ah, there's a bloke who knows what's what!" the down-and-out said, his voice oddly gentle for a moment. "Yeah, mate, we both know the score, eh?"

The moment of tranquility passed and the man resumed his tirade at the two police officers and one male nurse who were trying to keep him under control. Cursing and yelling in protest, he was eventually dragged out of sight. A white-haired senior nurse who happened to be passing clucked in disapproval, looked down at Mike.

"Don't let them psych you out, dear, they're all saying crazy stuff," she said. "I mean, even crazier than usual. We've had so many of them in these last few weeks, causing trouble. Weird thing is, none of them seem to be on booze, drugs, anything. It's like they're being fired up by something we can't detect."

The nurse started to walk away.

"Excuse me," Mike said, "but—I know this sounds bonkers—but is there any pattern to the way these homeless people act? Are they picked up near a particular place? Or something like that?"

The nurse frowned, walked back to Mike, and leaned down, spoke more softly.

"You didn't hear it from me," she said, "but I heard they tend to act up most when there's a TV crew around. I suppose you'd expect that, in a way, but it's odd that they always seem to zero in on the nearest camera. And the town is full of reporters these days, what with all the fuss about—you know, the asylum and stuff."

"Thanks," Mike said faintly as she left the waiting room.

Getting Palmer more publicity, keeping the pot boiling, he thought. *The more attention he gets, the stronger and more confident he becomes. Okay, but what's his endgame?*

Mike decided to ask the receptionist about Paul again and, if there had been no change, to go home for some shuteye. Before he was halfway to the desk, his phone vibrated. Fearing Ella had suffered a relapse, he checked it at once. It was a call from Farson. Mike played it, and heard nothing at first but some vague noises that might have been a man gasping or sobbing. Then, with startling intensity, a piercing howl erupted from the speaker.

"Jesus Christ!" he exclaimed.

Mike held the phone away from his head as the agonized noise continued. People sitting nearby looked around. Mike killed the sound then stood for a while, unsure what to do next. Suddenly self-conscious, he went out into the hall and tried to call Farson back. The detective's phone went straight to voicemail. Mike wondered if he should simply call the police and report what had happened, but reasoned this could get Farson into trouble.

Or into even more trouble, he thought. *Bugger, what am I supposed to do?*

Mike suddenly felt very much alone. He considered calling Neve Cotter, who knew the situation and could be trusted. But as he pondered the situation, he concluded that there was probably nothing she could do. This left only John Beynon, who was undeniably an expert on the paranormal, but hardly trustworthy.

"Sod this," he muttered, setting off toward the main entrance. "If I don't sleep, I'll collapse like Paul. Not much use to anyone then."

***

"It's anger, Ella—anger can do it. Fear is what keeps us stuck here."

Paul looked down at the girl, trying to hold onto his rage against Liz, against Palmer, against the wild injustice of it all. Ella seemed skeptical, and very much afraid. Paul tried not to feel any anger at her, aware of how much worse things might become if the Rookwood scenario played out. He had been in Liz's mind too often to believe that simple confinement was all this hell could bring. Whatever this nightmare world was, it somehow contrived to dissect the worst aspects of someone's nature and fling the resulting horrors back at them. He tried to explain that to Ella.

"Listen to me," he said, reaching down to clutch her hand. "Anything we fear or hate about ourselves will—will be real here, but only if we let it. One emotion can swamp another, overcome it. We have to be angry, I think, but in a focused way. Can you do that?"

Ella nodded, but Paul wondered if she was genuinely convinced.

The padded cell shimmered and darkened again. Still trying to cultivate his anger, direct it against the netherworld around them, Paul also struggled to grasp what might be happening.

What if this place is unstable? he thought. *This isn't our world. Neither of us has suffered Liz's torments.*

It explained why, what had been a vast labyrinth of mirrors had shrunk to this one room. An even more disturbing thought struck him.

What if it disintegrates, and takes us with it? What happens to our minds, our souls, if we don't escape back into the world of the living?

Paul looked around him. Already the padded walls were showing signs of decay, great rents appearing in the fabric, a foul liquid flowing down the walls. The single light bulb dimmed, faded to a glowing orange filament, then came back to hesitant life. Paul heard Ella whimper, felt her clutching his hand more tightly.

"You're a brave girl, I know you are. Don't let fear win. Conquer it, focus on your anger, Ella."

"I can't!" she wailed. "I'm too scared."

God, I'm an idiot, Paul thought. *She's a kid, not some kind of goddamn hero.*

"Okay," he said hastily, as the light dimmed again. "Here's another idea. Think of your mother, how much you love her. You can do that, right? Cling to that feeling, focus on your mom."

Ella nodded, closed her eyes, and bowed her head. Paul pinned his hopes on the pure, powerful emotions of a child, hoping he was right. Liz had been an adolescent, and a much abused one. Ella, he felt sure, was more balanced, and her relationship with Neve must be a good one.

As if to confirm Paul's theory, a face appeared in the gloom. It was Neve Cotter, fiery hair disheveled, apparently asleep. The woman's face grew larger, and Paul saw her eyelids flickering. He reached out and simply shouted to try and gain her attention. Neve's head turned, mouth open, as she seemed to come close to wakefulness.

Then Liz's face appeared, blotting out Neve's. It was a vile face, barely recognizable as a young woman, grotesquely contorted with a desperate rage far more intense than anything Paul could muster. He felt Liz's power as she lashed out at them, stung their mind with pain. The dead girl's huge, dark eyes seemed to fill the dimly lit room. Her mouth moved, shaping a single word.

"*No!*"

Ella screamed and flung herself against Paul, clinging silently to him and quivering. Liz vanished again, but refusal to help them seemed to echo to infinity.

***

Neve Cotter returned home to find her mother sitting up, watching TV with the subtitles on and the sound turned down. It was a Swedish crime drama, a convoluted serial killer story set in a bleak Scandinavia, where winter never seemed to end. Neve plumped down heavily on the couch, kicked off her shoes, sighed.

"Is she okay?" she asked.

"Oh, aye, she's fine—sleeping like a baby," replied her mother.

Neve sensed something odd in her mother's voice. Mary Cotter's face was impassive in the flickering light from the TV screen. But the woman shifted uncomfortably under her daughter's scrutiny.

"Come on, Ma, what's up?" Neve asked.

"Nothing, I'm just tired," replied the older woman. "All this strangeness—I never would have believed in such things. Where will it end? What'll become of that poor American fella? Oh, I give up."

Mary got up and stretched, then looked down at her daughter.

"I think we should both get some shuteye, don't you?"

"Sure," Neve said, heaving herself upright. "I'll take the couch."

Neve stopped her mother less than a minute later as Mary headed for the main bedroom.

"Ma, what is it, really?" she demanded, keeping her voice low. "Don't keep your opinions to yourself, that'll break the habit of a lifetime."

"Oh, you," Mary said, in mock outrage, giving Neve a little slap on the shoulder. "It's nothing. I just... it's as if Ella's had something taken out of her, you know? I mean, it's probably just tiredness. But when I tucked her in, I asked her if she wanted a night light, and she looked blank. Then she said yes, but I could tell she'd had to think it through. As if she wasn't scared of the dark anymore."

Neve thought it over. She often resented her mother's interventions over her parenting, but when Mary was genuinely worried, she could hardly ignore it.

"Well, maybe she isn't so scared," she said finally. "Paul took the hit on her behalf, kind of. Poor guy. It probably is tiredness, anyhow. Let's wait and see in the morning."

Neve pulled out the sofa-bed and arranged some sheets, then went to clean her teeth. On her way back from the bathroom, she glanced into Ella's room through the half-open door. Ella was laying on her side, curled up, her head barely visible above the duvet. Neve smiled, thinking that was normal enough. It was only as she pulled the covers up to her chin and wriggled to try and get comfortable that something odd struck her.

She was sleeping on her left side, surely, not her right?

For a moment, Neve doubted her own memory, and the matter nagged at her until she went back to check. But now Ella had completely vanished, only a girl-sized bulge under the duvet was visible. Neve felt a momentary impulse to go and check, see if her recollection was wrong. Then she went back to the living room and lay down again.

Okay, she might have changed her sleeping habits, maybe—so what? She's a twelve-year-old girl. My baby girl will soon be a teen. Lots of changes in store.

Neve eventually fell into a fitful doze. A recurring dream haunted her, in which Paul and Ella reached out to her. They were in some kind of room, a filthy, cramped space that Neve felt she knew, but could not recall. She kept waking up, turning over, trying to sleep again. By the time morning came she was exhausted and miserable but forced herself to get up and start making breakfast.

"Don't worry, love, I'll do that," said Mary, padding into the kitchen and yawning broadly. "Dear me, I had a restless night. Hope Ella slept better. I'll get off home straight after breakfast, let you get on."

The two women stood awkwardly for a moment, then Mary asked an obvious question.

"Isn't she up yet?"

"No," said Neve, feeling tension rise. "No, she isn't."

"Normally, you can't keep her in bed," Mary pointed out, and shook her head sadly. "She must be exhausted, poor thing."

Neve poured herself a cup of coffee, keeping her back to her mother.

"Yes," she said. "That must be it."

***

Mike Bryson woke early after a restless night and found that even limited sleep could birth an idea. It occurred to him that simply enquiring after Farson would not arouse suspicion, given the detective had spoken to him in a legitimate investigation. But when he called police headquarters, he was simply told the detective was not available.

"No, I don't want to leave a message, thanks."

Mike stared at his phone, wondering whether to try Farson again, then decided to check up on Paul instead. The official message was that there was no change in the patient's condition. Mike, with a day's work ahead of him, tried to focus on the next few hours, putting the more important matter on hold. He sent Neve Cotter a text message with the 'no change' report, then took a shower.

Preoccupied, unsure of what he might usefully do, Mike decided to simply shave and get off to work early. He reached out to wipe the condensation from the mirror above the basin, then stopped. There were a few apparently random streaks on the misted glass. Already, they were fading, as Mike had opened the bathroom window. He rushed to close it, turned to see the last vestiges of three words.

WE IN HELL

For a wild moment, he wondered if he might have written the words himself, lack of sleep finally driving him over the edge. But then he recalled the messages written on the walls of Rookwood, words etched in blood on fresh plaster. From this, it was a short leap to conclude that Paul might be responsible.

But why 'we'? Why not simply 'In Hell'?

Mike asked himself the question a dozen times over the course of the morning. The only answer he could come up with struck him as crazy. At first.

CHAPTER 9

"This might be—kind of a good thing, in a way."

Ella looked up at Paul. He felt a pang of guilt at the sudden hope in her face. She was a child, he reminded himself. For all her undoubted intelligence, for all she had faced, things no child should experience, she still believed adults were wiser. She trusted him, now, because there was precisely one grown-up to cling to, and it was Paul Mahan.

"What do you mean?" she asked.

"Well," he said, gesturing at the gloomy little cell. "We're together, right? Somebody once said that one and one is more than two."

Ella looked confused and a little dubious.

"What that means is, people can be braver when they have somebody to be braver with. Kind of."

Ella nodded, but he still saw doubt in her expression. The quiver of her lower lip belied the direct gaze from her gray-green eyes. She was just barely holding it together.

"And there's another thing," he added, trying to shape half-formed thoughts into words. "When Liz was trapped here, she saw her own personal nightmares—all the bad things about herself. Things she feared, hated. Her every weakness reflected in those distorting mirrors. Right?"

Ella nodded, silent, still staring up at him.

Land the goddamn plane, he told himself. *Before she loses it.*

"But now we're together here, in the place that shows one person their biggest fears, their worst nightmares, right?"

Another nod, the small face still looking closely at him, searching for both truth and reassurance.

"So, our fears can't be exactly the same—these things are always personal, unique to the individual."

He saw enlightenment dawn on her pinched, pale face.

"Everybody has different fears," she said slowly. "So this place can't really make us afraid. There can't be one thing that would be the worst thing in the world for both of us."

"Right!" he exclaimed in relief. "The worst thing it could do would be some kind of cheesy, old-school scare—like a haunted house at a carnival, something like that. And whatever happens, we both know it's not real, right?"

Ella nodded, but then the smile died on Paul's face when he saw doubt reappear on hers.

"But maybe there's something we're both very, very scared of?" she said, voice just above a whisper.

Noises, faint at first, began to echo outside the cell door. Paul knew there was a corridor out there, poorly lit, walls painted a sickly green. Walls devoid of pictures, of anything bright or hopeful. Not the walls of a modern institution, a place of healing. No, out there was Rookwood Asylum as it had been, the place where Liz and so many others had been tormented.

The domain of Doctor Miles Rugeley Palmer.

"Yeah," he said hastily. "But the thing is, if—if he comes, it's not the real him, is it? I mean, the real—the real one is out in the world, causing trouble in Tynecastle, following some crazy plan of his own. We're not trapped in his world."

Ella looked away, stared at the door. She put her hands over her ears as the noise from outside grew in volume. Shrieks, howls, clashing doors, the rattling of laden trolleys over tiled floors. The asylum was fully occupied, a working mental hospital, an instrument of Palmer's will. Palmer, whose name Paul did not dare pronounce, much as people in olden times had been afraid to mention the Devil, lest they conjure him up.

"He can't be here, that's—that's not how it works," he said, but he failed to convince himself.

Hands still clamped over her ears, Ella thrust her face down, against her knees, tried to make herself small in the corner. Paul moved closer to the girl, put a protective arm around her, gaze fixed on the door. He started when the small viewing hatch slid aside with a sharp snap. A pair of spectacles glinted within the black rectangle. The hatch closed, and he heard the rattle of a bunch of keys.

Then Doctor Palmer opened the door.

***

"Do come in, Mike—I'll just close up shop. Any passing horde of book-crazed consumers with money to burn will just have to go and bother someone else."

Beynon reversed the sign in the doorway. It no longer informed passersby that the shop was *Open To Browsers*. Now it apologized— *Sorry! Books Need Rest, Too!* The attempt at quirky good humor seemed a little sinister to Mike as he followed Beynon through the heavy-laden shelves and upstairs to the cramped apartment. As he climbed the steep, narrow stairs he thought he saw movement from the corner of his eye, a furtive shifting of shadows. But when he looked directly into the gloom at the back of the bookstore, he saw nothing.

"Tea?" Beynon asked, gesturing for Mike to sit down.

"Sure, milk, no sugar," Mike replied, not because he wanted tea, but to gain a little time to gather his thoughts. During his drive to Durham from Tynecastle, he had tried to work out a way to admit to Beynon that they had withheld information from him. Mike wondered if, given the arcane powers he had displayed, the old man might know anyway. He thought about the last message from Farson, who was still off the radar, which implied Beynon might be much older than he seemed.

Irrelevant, probably, Mike told himself. *Focus on the task at hand—saving Paul. And maybe Ella, too.*

"A friend in need is a friend indeed," said Beynon, bringing a tray through the bead curtain. "I would give it a few minutes for the tea to mass, as they say in these parts. Or brew, as we non-locals have it."

He set the tray, laden with teapot, milk jug, and cups, down on a low table next to a book. Mike had glanced at it earlier, but now—as Farson picked it up—he saw it was the volume that had brought him and Paul here in the first place.

"Yes! *Megapolisomancy*, in the flesh, so to speak," confirmed Beynon. "Here, take a look."

Mike took the book, examined its battered cover. He wondered why, if Thibault de Castries had been such a brilliant man, his book had evidently been printed on cheap paper between unadorned boards. The book had the look of a crank production. He checked the first few pages and saw it had been produced by Far Sight Press, a firm he had never heard of. As he turned the brown-edged pages further, one fell out.

"Sorry," he said, replacing the leaf. "I suppose it's been read to death down the years, by would-be—what do you call them? Megapolisomancers?"

Beynon gave a quick hand clap. It did not seem to be ironic, but Mike was never quite sure how much mockery lurked behind the book dealer's genteel manner. He was even more conflicted, now, about asking for Beynon's help. But the man seemed to be the only available option.

"Excellent!" said the book dealer. "I just thought of myself as a seeker of hidden truths, but you have coined a much more striking term. Oh, would you like a biscuit, by the way? I have Garibaldi, Bourbon, Fig Newtons—perhaps even some that aren't linked to historical figures."

Mike took a breath.

"No, thanks, I'd rather just get down to it. I need your help with something—call it a side project, something we didn't mention before. Me and Paul, that is."

Beynon paused in pouring milk into the second cup, raised a quizzical eyebrow.

"Yes, where is Paul?" he asked. "I did think he might have been in touch by now. After all, you've both had time to peruse de Castries."

Mike launched into an explanation of where Paul was, physically, and why. He did not try to manufacture an excuse for keeping Beynon in the dark. Instead, he told the truth.

"To be honest, John, we tacitly decided we wouldn't trust you with sensitive information unless we had to. Need to know basis, all that stuff."

Beynon raised his hands in mock horror.

"You didn't trust a total stranger who dabbles in the occult? What on earth could have possessed you? Oh, I'm so offended."

Mike had to laugh at that, despite his misgivings about the man. Whatever else Beynon might be, he was not petty. He picked up his teacup, feeling he had to make a small a gesture of solidarity, then paused. The bead curtain leading to what Mike presumed was a kitchen area had shifted slightly. Beynon, head on one side, glanced over at the doorway.

"I may have left the bathroom window open," he mused. "Talking of which, your mirror-message is interesting. From this Liz girl's mirror hell to your home—achieved in one far from easy step, I imagine."

Mike nodded miserably. He had heard enough from Paul about the world Liz was in. Too much, in fact. And the Ella issue was a complicating factor that left him feeling even more impotent and ignorant.

"I think you're right," said Beynon, topping up his teacup. "Paul and this girl—Ella?—are probably victims of a deceptive paramental entity. One that played the role of victim, maybe was a victim in a sense, but seized the first opportunity to commandeer another's body."

Beynon gave a histrionic shudder.

"Truly awful. You have not confided your suspicions to the child's mother, you say?"

Mike explained that Neve had called him to ask about Paul's condition earlier, and he had given a noncommittal answer. Beynon agreed it was probably best not to alarm 'the poor woman', just in case Mike's suspicions were unfounded.

"But in the meantime," the book dealer said, "we need to find a way to rescue Paul, and that's interesting. It will require a lot more than the general principles outlined by de Castries, I'm afraid."

Mike heard the bead curtain stir again, looked around to see a shadow moving behind the colorful strands. It was a slender shadow, and stealthy. He heard no footsteps. Mike stood up, alarmed, wondering who might be listening in the next room. All his earlier doubts about Beynon resurfaced. The dealer remained seated opposite, holding his teacup, smiling slightly.

"Who's in there?" Mike demanded. "I thought we were alone. Do you live with someone?"

"We are alone," said Beynon quietly. "In one sense. We are the only two human beings in this flat. But, you're right, I do live with somebody. She's normally a little shy, but now she's seen enough of you to want to make your acquaintance."

Mike began to back away toward the door, not quite panicking, but feeling suddenly vulnerable. The small room seemed to close in, become even smaller. He reached behind him for the door handle, found it, but the door would not open. Beynon stood up, and with his free hand, fished a small bunch of keys out of his pocket, jingled them.

"Sometimes, the simplest methods are the most effective," he said. "Now, the good news is that I will help Paul, for my own reasons. The bad news—for you at least—is that my price is rather high."

Mike decided to try a grab for the keys and lunged forward. Fear made him clumsy, and he collided with the edge of the coffee table as he tried to grapple with Beynon. The older man stepped deftly away, not spilling a drop of tea. Too late, Mike saw Beynon thrust his foot out to trip him, and he fell into an old armchair. Winded, Mike staggered upright. Behind him, he heard the bead curtain rattle.

"Here she is," Beynon said casually. "The Dark Lady has been so eager to meet you."

Mike turned clumsily, holding up his hands to ward off the threat. The nebulous, dark form gliding toward him seemed to flow over his fingers, up his arms, and he felt an intense chill embrace his flesh. The hooded form seemed to be veiled, as all he could see in place of a face was a rippling surface of blackness, a not-quite-material substance somewhere between fabric and smoke. He managed to pull one hand free, lashed out. His fist passed through the figure's head with minimal resistance. Mike was thrown off balance and tumbled heavily to the threadbare carpet. Pain shot through one of his knees as he landed.

"It's easier if you just cooperate," Beynon remarked, looking down at him. "She knows you better than you know yourself. Go with it."

The night-black entity flowed down over Mike, covering his body, the dark vapor blotting out the shabby room. The hooded non-face was pushed into his, and he yelled for help. Cold flowed into his throat, and he found himself in a lightless world, paralyzed. Then he saw something, a faint glimmer in the darkness, seemingly far away. It grew closer, became a feminine face. It was an unbelievably beautiful face, the quintessence of everything Mike had always desired, but never believed he deserved. It smiled, and for a moment, his panic subsided.

Then the face grew, its mouth opened far wider than any human mouth could, or should, and it began to devour his mind.

***

Brockley Whins, like most politicians, had had plenty of practice looking interested in things he did not really understand. As the dean of the science faculty showed him around Tynecastle's computer research facility, he went through a careful checklist of responses. He looked thoughtful, impressed, amused, taking his cue from the dean's tone and expression. That was the easy part. The more difficult part came after the tour, when the TV news crew left and Whins spoke privately to the dean in the latter's office.

"I can see the Lovelace Unit is a world-class facility," he said. "But this wave of—unpleasant incidents. You're sure that you are providing as much support to your students as possible?"

The dean, a smooth bureaucrat of a type very familiar to Whins, reeled off a list of measures the university had put in place. The mental health of students, he insisted, was Tynecastle's first priority.

Making money is your first priority, Whins thought. *We both know that. And these suicides are bad for business.*

"I'm sure that is the case," he said, smiling. "But as Member of Parliament for this city, I find myself in the awkward position of defending your university against accusations of neglect. Mental health is a big issue these days, as you know. The government has made promises, commitments. Of course, these are unusual circumstances. But the allegation is that the extremely febrile atmosphere caused by the Palmer phenomenon, plus the pressure to excel regardless of cost, has driven some young men and women over the edge."

Quite literally, in some cases, Whins thought, rather pleased at his own cleverness.

The dean blustered a little, but Whins adopted a familiar tactic, posing as an ally of the man while undermining his confidence. By the time he had finished talking about government scrutiny and questions being asked in Whitehall, the dean was looking distinctly sweaty and flustered.

"The important thing is that you feel you can talk to me if anything else should happen. My door is always open, as they say. And I trust yours is, too?"

Whins took out his card and handed it to the dean, who looked at the cream-colored rectangle with a slightly stunned expression. For a moment, Whins wondered if the man was sensing something wrong, and started talking more loudly.

He must hold it for a few moments for a connection to be made, Whins recalled. *I'll distract him long enough.*

"Now, that's my personal number, not my office," Whins said, standing up. "And that means you can give me a call anytime if any further—unpleasantness requires a response for me. I really do want to defend you against all this unreasoning criticism. Please, keep that card close to you."

The dean, showing him out, seemed pathetically grateful. Whins got into his town car and ordered the driver to take him back to his apartment. Then he took out his phone and texted Beynon. The book dealer called immediately.

"He took the card? Held onto it for at least ten seconds?"

"Yes," Whins replied. "I felt rather like a conjurer, making sure he got the right one."

"So long as he physically touched it for long enough, that should let us obtain the security data. That's our way in," Beynon said, somewhat smugly. "So glad it's simply a question of a numeric code. I'll wager they don't change it too often, either. Always the way with these places. Sloppy."

Whins frowned, looked out of the tinted windows at the street. A sudden burst of autumn sunshine illuminated lunchtime crowds of shoppers, people queueing for coffee and sandwiches, individuals smoking in alleyways.

"You mean it's your way in, surely, Beynon?" he asked finally. "I don't need to be there at all. That was never mentioned. It's not as if I can do anything. Surely I'd be in the way."

There was a pause, then Beynon spoke again, not in his usual urbane voice, but in a clipped, commanding tone.

"You will be there, Mr. Whins, because I say you will. The presence of a former government minister might just give us an edge should some officious security guard barge in. I must go, I have an important experiment to perform."

Before the MP could protest, the call was ended. He stared at his phone for a few moments, then put it back into his pocket.

***

Neve Cotter drove her daughter home from school at three forty-two. It was a fifteen-minute journey, minimum, usually longer due to the heavy school-run traffic. For the first few minutes Neve said nothing, mindful of the ritual whereby Ella would speak when she felt like it, talk about her day if she felt like it. But after five minutes Neve began to wonder if Ella was going to say anything.

"You okay, hon?" she asked, glancing over at the girl after stopping for a red light.

Ella was peering at the people on the sidewalk, almost gawping as if there was something remarkable about the small shopping precinct. She turned to face her mother, smiled.

"Yes, Mummy, I'm fine. I'm just a little tired, still. Because of all that trouble with Liz."

Neve nodded, and was about to say something about Paul, then stopped herself. It was capricious, tricky, to wait and see if Ella said anything about the American. She knew he had been taken to the hospital and had heard nothing since.

She'll eventually ask, Neve thought. *She has to. She's a caring child, she has a lot of compassion.*

The light was green and someone behind honked impatiently. Ella hastily put her car in gear, and it jerked forward. Ella emitted a small squeak of alarm, her face showing clear panic. It was odd, as the girl had had plenty of experience with Neve's less-than-perfect city driving.

"Sorry, I suppose I'm a little frazzled after all the excitement," Neve said.

She waited for the girl to take the opportunity to ask about Paul, but again Ella remained silent.

"You forgot your phone this morning," Neve added "Not like you. Imagine being out of touch with Katie for all that time."

Ella's expression was inscrutable. She looked briefly at her mother but did not speak.

"Granny left a cottage pie," Neve went on, trying to sound normal. "You always like those, don't you?"

"Yes," said Ella. "I like cottage pie. It's lovely."

Somehow, Neve managed to park in a very tight spot just a few doors down from their apartment building. She got out, expecting Ella to do the same. But instead, the girl remained seated in the passenger seat until Neve walked around and opened the door. The girl then waited while Neve closed the door, looking up at her mother expectantly.

"Okay," Neve said, trying to sound bright and carefree. "Home again, home again..."

She waited for Ella's response, but none came. She reached out and took her daughter's hand, and the girl did not pull away. Trying not to tense up, not to walk too fast, Neve led the girl up the path, opened the front door, then led her up the stairs. She let go of Ella's hand at the door to their flat, and let the girl go in first. Watching Ella hang up her school blazer she felt a sudden impulse.

"Don't forget to take off your shoes!" she called as she took off her own, along with her jacket.

Ella looked slightly startled, but then complied, carefully placing her shoes in the corner behind the door, next to Neve's. Then the girl went into the living room and stood, hands by her side and looked at Neve, as if awaiting orders. Neve took a deep breath, feeling her heart pounding.

Once might be a mistake, a case of daydreaming, kid in a world of her own, she thought. *But not so many as this. So many in a row.*

Neve fixed a smile on her face as she entered the living room and waited for Ella to step aside. But the girl remained standing in the middle of the floor, midway between the TV and the sofa, blocking the way to the kitchen.

"You want to help me with the cottage pie, honey?"

"Yes, Mummy, I do," said Ella, and turned, took a step backward. "I can help from here."

Neve hesitated, puzzled, watching as Ella's eyes closed, her forehead wrinkled. She clenched her pale, pink-nailed hands in front of her plaid skirt. There was a sudden crash from the kitchen as the fridge door slammed open, flung right back against the wall. A Tupperware container floated out, wobbling slightly, then accelerated to a terrifying speed, hurled itself against the far wall. The lid was blown off and a mess of brown and white mush sprayed over the wall and then flowed down onto the floor.

"Jesus Christ!"

Neve covered her mouth with one hand, feeling bewilderment and terror.

"You were testing me," said Ella's voice. "I know there's no friend called Katie. I know Ella was a vegetarian. I'm not stupid, Neve. I was poor and innocent when I lived and when I died. But I was not stupid."

The girl sat down on the sofa, and the TV came on, blaring suddenly, filling the dimly lit room with reflected light. The remote sat, untouched, on the armchair opposite the girl. A quiz show was nearly over, a couple of contestants vying for the big prize. Neve stood, immobile, while the girl frowned as the questions were asked.

"There's a lot I don't know," she said, looking up at Neve. "But that doesn't matter. I'll learn to fit in quite quickly. I'll have a good life, now. The life I should have had. You're really nice, when you try, and you'll provide for me. You've got no choice, have you?"

Neve shook her head, retreated toward the door, no thought in her head but to get away. The door to the little hallway swung shut at ferocious speed, caught Neve's leg. She screamed and leaped aside as the door slammed shut. Ella's face was now turned toward the TV again.

"You can't do anything to me, or do anything about me," said the girl. "Because if you tell them the truth, they'll take me away from you, call you barmy. They do that when they think the mother is unfit to take care of her daughter."

The bitterness in her voice was horrifying. Neve walked slowly over to the armchair that faced the sofa, sat down carefully, afraid of what response any sudden move might trigger.

"That's sensible," said Ella's voice, as she continued to gaze at the game show. "We can get on all right. All I want is to live the life I should have had. Is that so bad? If I can't live it with you, maybe granny would be given custody after they put you away. Or a nice, middle-class foster family. There are lots of kind people in the world. And anybody who isn't kind, well..."

The TV changed channels, slowly jumping from station to station at first, then more rapidly, until the screen was a bewildering chaos of light and color. Then the quiz show was back.

"Liz —" Neve began, hearing the desperation in her voice.

The girl looked at her, then, and put a finger to her lips.

"No, I'm Ella now," she warned. "My name is always Ella, I'm your daughter. I'm twelve. I have had a lot of trauma lately. Don't make me angry with any of that nonsense. I'm a nice little girl, and I need lots of loving care and understanding."

The sound from the TV suddenly went dead, though the picture continued to cast its flickering glow over the girl.

"You don't know what it's like," the girl went on, her eyes no longer focused on Neve. "So long in the cold, in the shadows. The living—you just don't get what life is, the intensity, the—the beauty of it. This world, now, is so wonderful. So many opportunities, so many freedoms. And all you do is moan and say you're hard done by."

The girl stood and walked over to the kitchen door, stopped, and turned to look at the woman.

"It's so intense," said Ella's voice, as if confiding a great secret. "To feel, hear, breathe again—to really walk, to eat and drink. I'd have liked that cottage pie. But I'll clear it up, like a good little girl. Then we can have something else. How about fish and chips?"

Neve, still speechless, watched as her daughter's body walked out of the room and into the kitchen, her socked feet almost silent. She watched the girl clearly relish even the most trivial contact with matter, with the world, with life. She watched as the girl cleaned up the mess without touching it with her hands.

Then Neve put her shoes and jacket back on and went out for fish and chips.

CHAPTER 10

"Visiting hours," said the nurse, "are clearly posted on the hospital's website, and as you can see they are also—also clearly displayed..."

The nurse stood, looking puzzled, one hand outstretched toward a printed notice on the door of the Intensive Care Unit. Then she looked over at Beynon, who was holding up a finger in front of the woman's face. The finger slowly folded itself down into the man's fist, and Beynon dropped his hand to his side. Two doctors, talking cheerfully, rounded a corner and walked by. As soon as they had vanished around the next corner, Beynon spoke.

"Now, let's try that again," said the book dealer. "We would like to see our friend Paul, who is inside. Let us in, please."

The nurse stepped back through the half-open door, Beynon following, Mike bringing up the rear. Mike felt a weird detachment from the situation, with no sense of nervousness at them breaking hospital rules. He had noted this peculiar emotional deadness during their drive in from Durham but could not make anything of it. He was unable to feel worried or resentful, either.

We're going to help Paul, that's the main thing, he thought. *John's proved to be a good friend, after all. Silly of us to suspect him. A bit paranoid, really. After all, he was old Percy's best friend.*

They walked, not too briskly, past the desk where a bored-looking junior nurse was typing data into an online form. The nurse who had let them in walked over to her subordinate, explained that they had 'distinguished visitors' who must not be interrupted. Mike followed Beynon into the side room as the two nurses continued their conversation in low voices.

"I hope by the time anybody does anything official about our intrusion, we'll be done—one way or another," Beynon said. "But to be on the safe side, Mike, if you'll just guard the door, in case our dear old National Health Service suddenly discovers the art of thinking fast?"

Mike smiled, closed the door, leaned against it. He studied Paul, whose face was obscured by tubes. His friend's chest was also exposed, sensors taped to it as it rose and fell slightly, slowly. An array of machines on wheeled stands stood around the bed, so Beynon had to weave between them.

So agile for an old bloke, Mike thought. *He must look after himself. Perhaps I should give up bacon or something.*

A troublesome thought welled up, only to flounder and sink again into the fuzzy vagueness of Mike's memory. He could not really remember much about the last few hours, and it bothered him a little. He recalled going to Durham to ask for John's help and then driving them back to Tynecastle. But between those two journeys, what?

Mike shook his head, trying to clear it, but then stopped to stare. Beynon had taken off his jacket, dropped it on the floor. Then he unbuttoned his long-sleeved flannel shirt and removed it. Mike tried to make sense of what he was seeing as Beynon continued to strip.

The older man's skin was something like a map, but also resembled a jumble of astrological charts. Symbols, some familiar, but most baffling to Mike, crowded every square inch of exposed skin. He thought of notebooks he had doodled in as a boy, filling page after page with caricatures of teachers and friends, abstract symbols, band names, anything. The same chaotic jumble seemed evident here, almost. But not quite. The more Mike gazed at Beynon's tattooed flesh, the more he realized there was a pattern, in fact, a series of patterns, layer upon layer. It was hypnotic, fascinating.

"The things one does to further one's career," said Beynon, taking off his underpants. He was totally naked, now, yet Mike felt no sense of unease. He had absolute confidence in Beynon, who continued to talk amiably. "For what it's worth, I was sore for months, especially in a couple of tender areas. But it was worth it, believe me. Magic is largely about symbols, you see, and having such symbols inscribed on one's body is an ancient method of obtaining protection, among other things."

Mike could not think of anything to say. He merely felt a sense of wondering admiration for this remarkable man, who had endured so much to become enlightened, and was now using his great ability to help a relative stranger.

So lucky to find him, Mike thought. *If only we'd contacted him earlier...*

Beynon began to speak, muttering syllables under his breath. Mike felt the temperature in the room drop, and saw breath start to cloud the air in front of Beynon's mouth. He was chanting, Mike decided, and the chant was somehow counterpointing the electronic notes from the machines. The chill grew more intense and Mike wrapped his arms around himself, shuddered. Yet Beynon did not seem bothered by the cold, despite his nakedness.

Then Mike noticed something stranger than the cold. The marks on Beynon's skin were moving. Symbols rotated, shifted sideways, grew or shrank. The patterns he had seen before changed moment by moment, an impossible waltz of bizarre geometries. At the same time, a shadow fell across the bed. Paul stirred. Mike recognized the form that had appeared above his friend, was lying on top of him, almost obscuring him with its dark presence. Suddenly Beynon raised his voice, lifting his hands above Paul and the flowing, rippling shadow.

"Consummatum est!"

The living shadow vanished. Lights flickered as the machines around the bed began to emit louder sounds. Mike saw flat lines, the red flash of warnings. From outside he heard a piercing alarm begin to sound, women's voices. He felt panic, tried to frame a question, but could not speak. Beynon turned his head, smiled over his shoulder.

"Give it a little time, these things are not accomplished easily."

"But—but he's dying!" Mike stammered.

Beynon was about to speak, but then the door hit Mike in the back as the two nurses rushed in.

"Who the hell are you?" demanded the ward sister who had tried to bar them earlier. Then, to her companion she said, "Call security! And for Christ's sake, will you put your clothes back on?"

"Your humble servant, madam," said Beynon, with an ironic bow, and he started to collect his clothes from the heap on the floor.

***

Again and again, the nightmare came for them. The keys rattled in the lock, the door swung slowly open, and Palmer stood there. A dumpy figure in a white coat, a furry caterpillar mustache on his upper lip, old-fashioned spectacles magnifying pale, watery eyes. Paul knew he should find the little man absurd, laugh at him, defy him. But he could not speak, or move.

It's a dream, a fantasy, it's not real.

But he could not persuade himself of that, not with the man who had inflicted so much suffering on so many helpless innocents standing before him. Not with the terrified girl pressing her face into his side, gripping him so tightly with her shackled arms. Not with the stench of carbolic acid and human excrement wafting in from the corridor. Not with the screams of the forlorn echoing through Rookwood, through his head.

"Ah, Paul, it's been a long time," said Palmer, stepping inside. "And I see you have a young friend. Let's start with her. The young always present simpler challenges, I find."

Two faceless orderlies entered the room. They were literally faceless under their masks, no features showing on the fleshy oval below their hairlines. What remained of Paul's reason told him their identities were irrelevant, that many—perhaps most—of those Palmer enslaved to his will were, to him, mere components, stripped of all individuality.

"Come now, it's easier if you co-operate," Palmer said in a light, conversational tone. "We have so much to get done! Such a long waiting list for treatment!"

The faceless men strode over to the cowering inmates. Ella began to scream plaintively. Paul tried to stand up, despite the restraints at wrists and ankles holding him within a foot of the wall. The first attendant simply shoved him in the face with a gloved hand and sent him reeling. He tried to hold onto Ella, but the other faceless man was already sweeping up the girl with immense, brutal strength. Paul grappled with the first orderly, who pushed him aside and unfastened the girl's manacles. He lunged forward, clutching desperately at Ella as she was dragged away, her howling and kicking ineffectual against her inhuman captors.

"We'll be back for you shortly, Paul," said Palmer.

"You bastard!"

And then the door was closed again, and Ella was beside him, and the viewing hatch opened to reveal Palmer's gimlet eyes. The cycle had been going on forever, or so it seemed, as Paul was in a world without sleep, without day or night, where time had ceased to mean anything. Repetition was madness, an insane ritual, breaking down the minds of man and girl. The fear of what was to come overwhelmed them again. Instead of reflections in mirrors, they were trapped in eternal dread.

How can I change this? How can I break the cycle?

Paul's exhausted mind struggled with possibilities. He could not fight the orderlies. He had tried shouting obscenities at Palmer. He had demanded to be taken instead of Ella. He had tried sarcasm, sneering, belittling the doctor. He had offered his soul in perpetuity if Palmer would simply free Ella. Nothing had worked. It was as if he were dealing with robots. Palmer's script was always the same, he made no response to any plea or abuse.

Keys rattled. There was a scraping as the door was unlocked. Palmer stood there again, dumpily real in this hell. As the diminutive doctor entered the room, Paul decided to play possum, make no move or sound. He had tried it before, to no effect, but he was determined to do better this time. He would head-butt the first orderly in the gut or gonads, try to send him reeling into the other, attempt to put the chain of his restraints around the neck of one, if they actually fell...

"Ah, Paul, it's been a long time."

The words were so familiar he had ceased to really hear them. But when Palmer stopped talking, Paul looked up, puzzled. The doctor was standing in the doorway, motionless. The only sound, now, was Ella whimpering quietly. The dim-lit cell began to waver and fade, the walls melting away. Paul looked down at his hands and saw they were no longer shackled. He no longer wore the stained, threadbare garment of an asylum inmate.

'Come.'

He was standing, dressed in his own clothes, in a room that looked familiar. He recalled Beynon's apartment in Durham, the comfortable worn furniture, the window with the view of the cathedral.

'Come.'

The speaker was a woman, dressed in a black robe. Her face was very pale, seemingly bloodless, and her eyes were vast pools of darkness. Her expression was blank, her hair two black wings that reached down to her shoulders. Her mouth seemed oddly small, like a scarlet bee-sting. And when she spoke, her tiny lips barely moved.

'Come.'

She reached out a hand and he took it, moving automatically as in a dream. He felt cool fingers grasp his, a gentle pressure, and she led him over to the battered sofa. Paul looked down at a young-ish man with a pleasant, slightly lined face. The man was sleeping, or perhaps unconscious. The woman leaned over and pressed her lips to the sleeping man, then stood up and pressed herself against Paul. As the small, cool mouth touched his, Paul finally grasped that *he* was the sleeping man.

A searing pain shot through him, and the commonplace living room vanished amid a glare of white light that made him flinch, cover his eyes. The last thing he heard as the pale radiance overwhelmed him was the seductive voice speaking one sentence.

'You will serve the greater purpose.'

***

Beynon and Mike allowed themselves to be escorted out of the ward but insisted that Paul had no next of kin in the UK, so only his friends were going to be available. They were allowed to stay in the waiting room, on sufferance. After the chaos had subsided, a senior doctor emerged to tell them that Paul had made a remarkable recovery.

"From a condition you couldn't identify in the first place," Beynon put in. "Very remarkable. You must be so pleased the bed will be freed up. Now, when can we take him home?"

The doctor, who was very tired and tetchy, seemed to ponder getting security back to eject the two men. But Mike intervened, expressing gratitude for how much had been done for his friend and asking if they could maybe have a legitimate visit this time? After ten minutes of backstage debate, they were ushered into Paul's room under the watchful eye of the ward nurse.

Paul was sitting up, looking tired and washed out, but alert. He smiled broadly when he saw Mike, and after a little hesitation, they shared a hug. Beynon hung back at the door, looking on benevolently.

"What the hell happened?" Paul asked.

Mike tried to explain what he had seen. Paul looked over at Beynon, smiled broadly.

"God, I owe you my life!" he exclaimed, holding out his arms.

"You're welcome," Beynon replied, walking over. "Pardon me if I don't hug, I'm a little old-school in that regard. But let's have a nice, firm handshake."

Mike saw Paul look slightly puzzled as he took Beynon's hand. It seemed as if his friend was struggling to recall something. When Mike asked, Paul confirmed that his memories were fragmentary at best.

"I remember this—woman? Maybe. And there was Palmer, and a

girl—I mean a child..."

"Might it have been Ella Cotter?" asked Mike anxiously.

"Ella?"

Paul frowned, concentrating, but then shook his head.

"It's all fading away. I can't tell which are memories of my—coma, or whatever it was, and memories of what happened before that. But what about Ella? Has something happened to her?"

Mike shrugged, again feeling the odd numbness, that unaccustomed emotional distance from other people. But every time he started to question what had changed recently to make him feel strange, a barrier arose in his mind. All he knew was that Beynon had saved Paul, and they should both be grateful to such a brilliant, selfless man.

"No," Paul said finally, "I can remember going to see Ella, and her mother and grandma, and you were there... But after that, nothing."

Paul slumped back into his pillow, and suddenly seemed like an old, tired man to Mike. The Englishman tried to imagine what his friend had gone through, then decided it might be best if he never knew the details.

"You need to rest, old chap," Beynon put in, laying a hand on Mike's shoulder. "Come, let's go and get a cup of foul coffee from a machine, and leave our friend here to rest. I, for one, always feel that simply getting a good night's sleep is—"

Beynon stopped, hesitated at the door he was opening for Mike, then seemed to recover. Mike felt a moment of concern for his friend. It suddenly occurred to him that, in saving Paul, the occult expert might have expended much of his own vital energy. Mike only had the vaguest idea how such things worked.

"Are you all right, John?" he said anxiously, putting a hand on Beynon's arm.

The other man's eyes were unfocused, but then he looked at Mike and smiled urbanely.

"Of course I am! Just a brief moment of—well, call it insight. An epiphany."

Seeing Mike's puzzlement, Beynon laughed briefly and ushered the other man out of the room.

"Suffice to say, I finally obtained some useful information earlier today, and now I find I must put that data to use a little sooner than expected."

As they left the Intensive Care Unit, Beynon explained to Mike that the enemy was finally moving toward the prime target. Mike, confused, asked if he could do anything to thwart Palmer's plans, whatever they were.

"Oh yes," said Beynon. "You and another key player in this rather complex game. The two of you are going to play a decisive role, rest assured."

Mike felt a sudden surge of pride at the thought that such an exceptionally gifted man would let him be front and center in his plans. He felt pleased with himself at having contacted Beynon in the first place, despite Paul's reservations.

Sometimes, he's a tad too cautious, Mike thought. *A little too averse to taking a risk, especially for an American. But, of course, he's been through the wringer since this whole thing began. You can't really blame him.*

CHAPTER 11

Neve Cotter sat at the kitchen table, staring down at her now-cold fish and chips. In the living room, the living, breathing body of her daughter sat on the sofa, an empty carton by her side. The girl had finished her meal and was now gazing in rapt attention at a nature documentary. It was, Neve thought, just the kind of thing that Ella would have liked. Anyone who knew them, just walking into the room, would assume everything was normal.

Oh God, what am I going to do?

The girl looked around. Ella's face was blank, the familiar pale, gray eyes unblinking. Then Ella's mouth smiled, chilling Neve with the unnaturalness of the expression. Ella had never smiled like that, a slightly crooked smile that suggested something was being held in reserve, that the mind behind it was hiding something. A secret nobody would want to know, if they valued their sanity.

"Mummy," said Ella's voice. "Can I have a cup of tea, please?"

"Of course... darling," Neve said, getting up.

She switched on the kettle, put a teabag in a mug. Then a question occurred to her. Without looking around at the living room door, she asked, "Milk and sugar?"

"Milk and two sugars, please, Mummy," came the reply.

Ella had never drunk tea or coffee before. Neve wondered what she would say to her mother when all the inconsistencies, the things that made little sense, triggered the inevitable questions. Mary Cotter would notice something was wrong, if not with Ella, then with Neve. She paused, suddenly horrified at the thought of what might happen if Mary said or did something wrong, if she made Liz nervous.

We'll have to go away, move somewhere, she thought. *Somewhere nobody knows us, so nobody can spot the mistakes Liz will keep making. We have to find a place where a twelve-year-old girl can sometimes talk like a teenager who died in 1955.*

Neve looked down as her trembling hand spilled a heap of sugar onto the countertop. She reached up with her other hand and clutched her wrist, forced herself to behave. She took deep breaths, and by the time the tea had brewed, she took it into the living room with a steady hand, laid it on a small table by the girl's elbow. Neve did not look the girl in the eye.

"Thanks, Mummy," Ella's voice said. "But you don't have to stay in the kitchen. Come and sit by me."

Trying to suppress her panic, her horror, Neve went to the kitchen doorway, switched off the light, and returned to the couch. She sat down gingerly, just far enough away from the girl so they didn't touch. Out of the corner of her eyes, Neve saw a small hand reach out, braced herself for the contact of familiar flesh that had somehow turned traitor.

On the TV, a huge shark appeared from the blue gloom and took an immense bite out of a fat, unwary fish. Blood, black in the depths, flooded the screen. Neve felt the small hand close more tightly on hers and tried not to think about it.

"So much life in this world," said Ella's voice.

How long before it doesn't sound like Ella anymore?

The thought struck Neve like a hammer blow. Her daughter would be lost to her forever, and the world would merely see a rather odd child entering her teens, growing up, leaving home to seek a life of her own. And, all the while, Neve would have to play the loving mother, somehow fend off Mary, and keep everything on an even keel.

I'll go insane.

***

"Let me in or I'll arrest you for obstructing a police investigation!"

Paul was jerked out of a light doze by a familiar voice. Farson was shouting down at least two nurses. A moment later, the detective burst into the room brandishing his ID at the irate ward sister. He was also disheveled and half-dressed, a dark raincoat hanging open to reveal hospital-issue pajamas.

"We've got to stop them!" Farson bellowed. "Come on, get your clothes on!"

"Who?" Paul asked.

"Beynon, Palmer, the Dark Lady!" Farson said, as if the answers were obvious. "It's all part of the same pattern."

Paul tried to focus on what was being said as Farson hustled him out of bed and shoved his clothes and shoes at him. But it was difficult, his mind was fuzzy. Beynon was an ally, surely? Percy's old friend, who had brought Paul back from hell, or something very like it. He began to explain this to Farson, who cut him off with a volley of expletives.

"He nearly killed me, or his pet demon did, or whatever the damn thing was. I was in—a bad place," Farson said. Paul saw a haunted look in the other man's eyes. "He tried to break me. But I survived. And, now, I'm going to take the bastard down."

Paul saw the detective's hand shaking, and the man's staring eyes. He did not want to contradict him and got dressed hastily. But he could not stop himself asking the obvious question.

"Where are we going?"

Farson was looking out into the corridor, evidently expecting problems. He replied without turning around.

"The place that's at the center of this case, the one place I never actually visited. The prime target. I'm sure—I just know it's the place."

Paul felt his doubts grow more profound but did not want to contradict the man. Besides, something gnawing at the back of his mind told him he was not seeing the whole picture, that he had been duped in some way.

If only Beynon was here, he thought, as he pulled on his jeans. *I'm sure he could set me straight.*

***

Neve caught movement at the edge of her vision, turned to look at the girl. Ella's face was frowning slightly. Neve felt her panic, never quite banished, rise again.

"Mummy, I think someone is coming," the girl said quietly. "Somebody not nice. Tell them I don't want to talk to them."

Neve began to ask what she meant when the door buzzer rang. She stood up, went to the intercom, and hesitated for a few moments. The buzzer sounded again.

"Tell them to go away, Mummy!"

Now Ella's voice sounded urgent, perhaps even a little afraid. Neve felt confusion, unsure what to do next. Then, as if her hand had a mind of its own, she pushed the intercom button.

"Who is it?" she asked.

"Mike," said a small, tinny voice, just recognizable as the English lecturer. "Can you let us in? I have someone who wants to talk to Ella."

"No, Mummy!"

Neve felt an invisible hand grip her wrist and jerk her away from the intercom. But it was too late, Neve had already pushed the Open button. Her own hand flew up and struck her, hard, on the side of the face. Another hand gripped her by the shoulder, clamping down like steel, and spun her around. Ella's body was standing up, somehow taller than seemed right.

"You let me down, Mummy! I'll punish you later, after I deal with these bad men."

Neve gasped as she saw her daughter's body was floating a few inches above the floor. The girl followed her gaze, shrugged.

"They know already, it doesn't matter."

The intense pressure on Neve vanished, and she staggered, trying to regain her balance. Ella's body drifted back, away from the door. The girl looked down at the sofa, which shifted slightly. For a moment, Neve was baffled. She realized Liz was afraid of someone, or something, that was approaching, wanting to get in. Neve's brain raced, struggling to make sense of the situation.

My enemy's enemy is my friend. Mike is a good guy, but it can't possibly be him she's scared of?

"Keep away!" the girl shouted, a note of panic in her voice. The sofa moved again, rolled over the carpet a few feet, but stopped short of the door.

"Help me, Mummy!" the girl shouted.

Neve looked at the door, then at her daughter's stolen body, thought of Ella's stolen life. She smiled to distract Liz, slow her reaction, then lunged for the door handle. A vicious blow glanced off her hip, making her gasp in pain, but she still managed to open the door and stagger outside.

Mike was just coming up the stairs, and his eyes widened in surprise when he saw her. Behind him was a stranger, an older man dressed in a long, dark coat, and a black polo neck. The door slammed shut behind Neve as she ran toward the stairs, trying to explain what had happened, who 'Ella' really was.

"We know!" said Mike, reaching out to her. "Everything's fine now."

Neve realized she was sobbing as she struggled to speak, and Mike was holding her close, patting her shoulder gently, speaking reassuring words. His companion, meanwhile, passed them with a hint of a smile.

"She's frightened, which makes her dangerous, Mike," said the stranger. "But it's also to our advantage."

Neve stared after the man as he walked up to her apartment door. The hall light had flickered on, sensitive to motion. But despite the illumination, it seemed as if the stranger had a huge shadow, one that flowed up the wall and moved independently. Then the man and the shadow were gone.

"Who is that?" she asked.

"A friend," Mike replied. "Beynon, an expert on all things occult."

"I thought you didn't—" she began, but then a child's scream came from inside her apartment. "Oh my God!"

Despite everything she had seen and heard, Neve could not fail to respond. She broke free of Mike, even as he shouted a warning for her not to interfere. She ran back down the hall, saw her front door was ajar, burst through it. Neve had not known what to expect. But what she saw astonished her.

The girl was standing quietly, looking up at the strange man. He no longer had a vast, improbable shadow. He looked rather like a kindly uncle visiting a favorite niece. Ella's face turned to Neve and beamed at her.

"It's all right, Mummy," she said. "I went away, and I was a little bit scared, but I'm all right now."

Neve hunkered down and grabbled Ella. It took her a few moments to gather her thoughts, look up at the stranger, let her mind work out who he must be.

"You're Beynon?" she asked. "Thank you! I owe you—everything."

The man shook his head in a self-deprecatory manner, and Neve felt herself resist the mannerism, and then the man. Although the evidence of his good intent was held close against her, warm and safe, Neve felt a sudden dislike for the book dealer. She felt the way she had when her abusive ex-boyfriend had offered her some treat or gift, that it was a trap designed to put her off balance.

"Neve," Beynon said, "I've only done half the job, you see. If I'm to keep your little girl safe, I need to destroy the menace once and for all."

Neve stared up as the man raised a slender, well-manicured finger in front of her face. She found herself staring at the light glancing from the nail, admiring the striations of the smooth oval. All her doubts washed away, and she felt a wonderful sense of confidence in Beynon. At last, she had found a man she could trust unreservedly.

"We need to go, now, Neve. And you must bring Ella."

"Yes," she said, standing up, and taking Ella's hand. "We must go."

A little apprehensive, but still filled with a sense of well-being, Neve and Ella followed Beynon and Mike downstairs, and out into the rain and the darkness of a late November afternoon.

***

"I don't quite understand..."

Brockley Whins waved the dean's protests aside and took him firmly by the arm. The MP ushered the college bureaucrat out of his office and along the corridor linking the admin block to the computer science faculty. Students passing the other way looked puzzled as the dean tried to smile and look normal but kept protesting under his breath.

"Please, put a sock in it, old boy," Whins said firmly. "We have an important rendezvous. This is a quantum leap in the density of our nation—indeed, in the world."

The dean began to explain that a quantum leap was, in fact, a very small jump, the smallest change possible. Whins stared down at the man, and his withering expression finally silenced him. They reached the entrance to the computer building and the dean saw three adults and a child waiting.

"Hurry, it will begin soon," said a thin, gray-haired man in black who seemed to be in charge. "Ah, this must be the top man, just in time to let us in."

"What's the meaning of this?" the dean demanded. "Who are these people?"

He looked from one face to the next. One of the strangers was vaguely familiar, a man in his thirties with an oddly tranquil expression, given the circumstances. The woman and the girl—evidently her daughter—also looked serene, which was disconcerting. The dean wondered if they were on drugs.

"Just open the door, please," said Whins.

"I will not! That's a secure facility and..."

The man in black raised one of his fingers, as if in gentle admonition. The dean stopped protesting and felt an overwhelming desire to unlock the door. He resisted, suddenly afraid that if he broke the rules, it would not merely be a bad mistake; that it might be something far more serious, something potentially fatal. He had never had a sense of incipient evil before, but, in the level gaze of the stranger, he felt he was confronted with something dark, inhuman, monstrous.

"No!" he croaked. "I—I have my duty—responsibilities."

The dean saw his hand slowly reach up and, with a series of painful jerky motions, punch in the numeric code. The door clicked open and the black-clad man led the others inside. Whins dallied for a moment, smiled smugly.

"I didn't believe he could do such things, either, at first," said the politician. "Oh, you might care to check your wallet."

Then the MP disappeared inside after the others. The dean stared as the door swung shut and clicked securely. Then, feeling a sense of unreality, he took out his wallet and checked it. There was nothing missing, nothing new. Then he found Whins' card and examined it. It had changed. The MP's name and contact details were obscured by a strange symbol, somewhere between a stylized snake and a curved dagger. The shape was hypnotic, disturbing.

"Sir, you need to get out of here."

He tore his gaze from the symbol to see a security guard looking anxiously at him.

"What? What is it? There are people—"

"I know, sir!" said the man impatiently. "A whole bunch of nutters are disrupting the campus. Hell, it's the whole center of the city, I reckon, but they seem to be focused on us. We can't cope, the police are snarled up in traffic."

The guard led the dean to the window. The dean realized he had been hearing muffled shouts and screams for some time. Outside, he saw flashing lights, a splash of orange flame, and shadowy figures running. A roar and clatter made him look up. The dean saw a helicopter overhead, searchlight jabbing downward. The intense light revealed chaos, a destructive rampage. The dean saw a man in ill-matched clothing with a disheveled mop of hair and an unkempt beard hurling a litterbin through a plate glass window. Then the searchlight moved on to reveal more violence, more apparently aimless destruction.

"What's happening?" the dean said, pleadingly.

"Oh, Jesus Christ," breathed the guard.

The dean saw it, too, a moment later. Against the backdrop of the rainy night, a greater darkness was rising. A colossal shape was looming over the university, and as the dean gazed up, open-mouthed with awe and horror, the police helicopter veered away like a panicked bird. The thing that was approaching might have been a tornado, towering incongruously above English city streets.

It might have been, except it was full of faces.

***

Paul felt his mind start to grow sharper, his thoughts and memories clearer, as they raced through the city center traffic. Farson had commandeered a car from a terrified young doctor, and now it sounded as if he were ruining the engine, suspension, and quite a few other components.

"You still haven't told me where we're going," Paul shouted, as he was hurled against the passenger door on a sharp turn.

"Where's the obvious place to become a god, these days?" Farson shot back. "Not in politics, the military, business—well, not regular business."

He cursed fluently for a few seconds as he overtook a slow-moving furniture van, then a bus whose passengers goggled at them as they shot ahead. Farson ran a set of red lights, causing a woman in a small car to screech to a halt and be shunted by a taxi. Horns blared, then the scene was behind them.

"The internet, Paul," Farson said, speeding up along a clear stretch of road, ignoring the shine of the rain-slick tarmac. "This all started with electrical therapy, or torture, whatever. All that stuff—megapolissycrap—it's right there in plain sight, for God's sake. Stupid not to see the link. Power to dominate others, to permeate the entire city, then the country, then, of course, the world wide web. Shit!"

Farson swerved as a woman ran into the street, and the car spun out of control. There was a sickening moment as the vehicle tipped up onto two wheels, then crashed down as the left front wing struck a parked car. Paul, winded, struggled to unfasten his belt. Farson was already climbing out, urging him to hurry.

"Look out!" Paul cried.

Farson turned just in time for an elderly woman to hit him on the side of the head with an empty wine bottle. The detective reeled but grabbed the woman's hand and kicked viciously at her legs, sending her sprawling. Paul was shocked by the violence, but then saw that other motley figures were emerging from the darkness, converging on them.

"Beynon's crazy militia, I reckon," Farson said, grabbing Paul's arm and hauling him out of the car. "Keeping the powers that be nice and busy."

Another bottle flew out of the night, smashed against the abandoned car. Enraged cries followed them as they dodged the disorganized mob by heading down a side-street, Farson's local knowledge proving useful. They emerged into an oasis of calm, a small urban square with a few straggling trees opposite the university. The men paused, getting their second wind. The campus seemed to be alive with activity, none of it normal. Abandoned vehicles, their doors open, were slewed across the road.

"Beynon?" Paul asked, bewildered. "Isn't Palmer behind all this?"

Farson grabbed him again, urged him onward.

"Same difference," he said. "That's my take on it. Beynon said something about planning this from way back. He's the son of that occultist, de Castries."

Paul began to protest, but the detective wasn't interested in a debate. He suddenly stopped, bent down, and picked up something from a mass of garbage littering the sidewalk. Paul saw it was a baseball bat, it's business end caked with something dark and sticky looking.

"Improvisation, great British talent," Farson muttered.

They crossed onto the campus, keeping to the shadows, taking an indirect route to the computer research facility. When they rounded a small theater, they stopped and stared at the vast, bizarre entity that had almost totally engulfed their destination.

The dark vortex was a whirlwind of faces, a storm of enchained souls. Each visage that whirled past was distorted by misery, pain, madness. Palmer was the ruler of his own personal hell, and at the heart of the black storm, they saw his face, smug and callous. Even as they watched, the vortex began to shrink, however. It seemed to drain away into the modernistic concrete building beneath it. The lights of the building went out.

"Too late!" Farson shouted. "Or maybe not."

He began to run, shouting over his shoulder for Paul to follow him. Paul did, his mind sharper than before, but still confused. He realized that Beynon must have used some kind of paranormal trickery on him, and on others. But the thought that the book dealer was de Castries' heir, that he had somehow contrived the entire situation, seemed preposterous.

Then a memory sprang into his mind. It was not, in fact, one of his own, but part of the panoply of memories he had experienced when he had merged briefly with Palmer. He had undergone the amoral little egomaniac's life as a series of jumbled flashbacks, many horrific or disturbing. But one had been utterly commonplace—the moment when a Tynecastle council committee had put Palmer in charge of Rookwood Asylum, not long after World War Two.

Paul saw the committee before him, the row of typical local politicians, unremarkable people trying to do their best. Except one, that is. One face stood out for its keen-eyed intelligence, along with its self-satisfied air. Beynon had looked a little younger back in the 1950s. But Paul could still clearly recognize him.

"Oh God, it was right there, but I didn't see it."

"Don't just stand there!" Farson reproached him. "Maybe we're not too late."

They raced for the blacked-out building and went inside. A door with a numeric security pad barred their way. Farson hefted his bat and swung.

CHAPTER 12

Neve had been afraid for Ella when she saw the disturbances unfolding in the heart of Tynecastle. But Beynon seemed to have some baffling power over the ragtag mobs of screaming, fighting, cursing individuals who were creating panic and disorder. She clutched Ella close at every crash, flinched when a petrol bomb exploded against the side of a police car. But after they could go no further in Mike's car, Beynon led them through the madness and onto the campus unmolested.

"It's like a fairy tale," said Ella, calmly. "They can't even see us, Mummy. There's nothing to be scared of."

Neve smiled down, reassured. Sometimes children made good sense. After they had entered the computer building, she felt herself relax, and took comfort in strong walls and windowless corridors. Even the presence of Whins, the creepy politician, did not really bother her. The chaos outside surely could not penetrate here. It was good of the book dealer to bring them to a safe place.

But we were safe before, weren't we?

The hesitant, small voice seemed treacherous, ungrateful to Beynon. But the thought worried her. Why had Beynon brought them here? Why bring a twelve-year-old girl into the middle of some kind of uprising? Beynon was yards ahead, striding quickly through a series of doorways, and she resolved to ask him just what his plan was. Neve was sure it was good and sensible, but...

The lights flickered, went out, then came back on hesitantly, though they failed to reach full brightness, as if most of their power was being drained. Beynon stopped on the threshold of yet another room. The door had an elaborate sign full of technical jargon. Some of the words felt familiar to Neve, but when she tried to recall what they meant, her mind became muzzy again.

"He's coming," said Beynon. "Right on cue."

The others followed him inside. Neve had expected something remarkable, a revelation that would miraculously explain all the strange, terrifying phenomena that had beset her and Ella. But all she saw were rows of metal cabinets, dark gray and unimpressive. There were desks, chairs, some other office paraphernalia, but nothing else.

"I know," said Beynon, smiling at her. "Our corporate planet in miniature. Flowing through this room is love, fear, hate, gossip, rumor—even a little genuine knowledge, the odd snippet of wisdom here and there. But mostly, of course, a staggering amount of hard-core pornography."

Neve's mind suddenly cleared, and she understood where she was.

"This is an internet node!"

Beynon gave a curt nod but did not speak. Instead, he seemed to be doing some kind of deep breathing exercise, his chest thrown out, arms braced. He was, Neve realized, preparing for some kind of ordeal. She grasped Ella's hand more tightly.

"Mummy?" the girl said.

Neve saw her own confusion and growing panic reflected in her daughter's eyes. She looked over at Mike. He was rubbing his eyes, peering around him like a man just waking from a baffling dream. Neve grasped that she had been hypnotized or otherwise controlled by Beynon, but that the man's grip had suddenly loosened.

"We need to get out of here," Mike said.

"I wouldn't try that," Whins warned, upending a desk and setting it up as a makeshift barrier in the corner of the room. "Time is very short."

The lights went out. Ella squealed in panic, clutched at her mother. In the pitch blackness, Neve saw that the gray cabinets were studded with small lights which flickered busily. The power drain had clearly not affected the system that funneled the whole area's internet through this room. She grasped that the Palmer entity was seeking to enter the web, become part of it, assume a kind of god-like status. But she could not see how that might benefit Beynon.

"We can still make a run for it," Mike began.

But the temperature was already falling, and a few seconds later their way out was barred by a cascade of distorted faces, mouths open in silent screams. Flashes of light, like miniature lightning bolts, played around the maelstrom of tormented souls. Neve retreated to the corner barricade, she and Mike trying to shield Ella with their bodies. Whins showed no interest in them, peering over the table, clearly anticipating something, but not noticeably afraid. After a few moments, it seemed the entity was not interested in them. Instead, the vortex focused on Beynon. Intermittent flashes of light showed the occultist was chanting, eyes closed, arms crossed over his chest.

Palmer appeared, his round, mustachioed face huge, taller than Beynon's entire body. This, Neve sensed, was the ultimate evolution of the entity, a being that had reached the peak of its power and was now determined to move on to a higher level. And all that seemed to stand in its way was Beynon.

Neve cringed, holding up one hand to minimize the painful intensity of the flickering light. Palmer looked down at Beynon, and the huge mouth opened, revealing a row of uneven teeth.

"Who are you to oppose me?"

Beynon did not stop chanting, but his voice rose a little, so that Neve could hear snatches of what might have been Latin, Greek, Arabic, or perhaps some mélange of those languages and many others. A tendril of blue-white light flashed out from the vortex of faces and played over Beynon's skin like St Elmo's fire. Neve flinched, expecting the man to collapse or burst into flame. But nothing happened. Beynon simply continued to chant, words tumbling out faster, his tone more emphatic.

Palmer's face flickered, seemed to dissolve into the surrounding blur of visages, before once more reforming. For the first time, the long-dead maniac looked hesitant, unsure of what to do next. Then Palmer's familiar, arrogant expression returned, and the vortex moved sideways, bypassing Beynon, and settled in the middle of the room. Filaments of light penetrated the dull gray cabinets.

"Oh God," said Mike, "he's going to take over—take control of it all!"

"No, he won't," said Whins, voice strained. "The plan is to take his place, destroy the mind of the thing, then use it. All it takes is a sufficiently powerful attack on the same psychic level."

In the intermittent light, Neve saw a small, slender figure appear by the door. A moment later, it was picked out again by the eerie blue flicker, much closer to Beynon. It was Liz, dark-haired, huge-eyed, still clad in the plain gray dress she had worn in her last days of freedom. Beynon unfolded his arms, held out his hands toward Liz. The two were motionless, ghost-girl and unnaturally old man. Neve wondered if Liz was striving to hurt Beynon, if the man was using all his powers to hold her in place.

She was just distracted enough that, when Whins snatched Ella out of Neve's arms, she did not react immediately. Whins heaved the girl over the table, out into the room. Neve screamed and grabbed at her daughter. Mike tried to grab the politician, but Whins was already out of their grasp. He ran past Beynon, past Liz, and tried to fling Ella into the heart of the Palmer entity. Neve, clambering over the barrier, heard her daughter screaming, but also saw Ella prove her presence of mind by grabbing onto Whins' arm and not letting go. The politician lashed out, and caught Ella a glancing blow, but the girl held on with both hands.

"Nooooo!"

Liz's scream went straight through Neve's mind as she began to run across the room. Neve fell to her knees, the pain of the psychic howl too much to endure. She glimpsed movement in the Palmer entity, saw three figures moving, two small and slender, one larger. The latter was suddenly cast aside, hurled against one of the metal cabinets with a crash and a shower of sparks. The others vanished.

"She'll fight for the body she needs," Beynon said casually, looking down at Neve. "And that will keep the old fool occupied. A distraction."

Mike lunged at Beynon, swung a fist, but the older man dodged effortlessly, then chopped down with a flattened hand. Mike collapsed, face down, unmoving.

"Thought I might need him," Beynon said, still utterly self-possessed. "I originally planned to overfeed him with too many deaths, including yours, in order to destabilize him. But the revised plan was better. More fun, too."

Neve did not think. She pointed at the doorway, eyes wide, screamed. Beynon turned, frowning, to look. In the moment the simple trick bought her, she punched him hard, between the legs. He doubled over, emitting a whoof of expelled air. She was on her knees, now, and hit him hard in the face with her fist. Feeling bones crack, wondering if one might be hers, she felt a cold joy in violence, in her sudden determination to kill this man.

She was trying to get upright to aim a kick at Beynon when he suddenly leaped back, out of range, and flung out an open hand, then slowly closed his fingers. Neve felt a tightness in her chest as if there were fingers clutching at her heart.

"You—you filth..."

A booming sound filled her head, then the floor came up and hit her in the face.

***

"Any actual plan, Nat?" Paul asked, as the lights failed. "Oh shit, that's great."

"Hang on," ordered Farson, and after a few seconds produced a flashlight. He handed it to Paul, hefted his bat with both hands.

"You're just going to try and smash him over the head, then?" Paul asked as they moved off again. The computer research facility was deserted, and Paul guessed the staff and students had sensibly fled when the rioting started.

"I'll do the violent stuff if you handle the mumbo-jumbo," snapped Farson. "You're obviously linked to all this, and Palmer couldn't finish you off. Either you're very lucky, or your link to Liz gives you some kind of immunity—limited immunity, maybe, but it's something."

"Oh, great," said Paul. "Some unspecified and unreliable defense against overwhelming evil."

Farson laughed at that.

"Smile, mate, you're a bloody hero!"

The screams came from nearby up ahead, and they began to run. Paul was not sure, but it sounded like a child and a woman. As they reached the door of the last room they heard confused shouting, another scream. Farson rushed in first and then froze. Paul pushed past him and saw the turmoil of faces, and Beynon facing the heart of the dark cyclone.

"Consummatum est!"

The old man's voice boomed out, his words seeming to echo eternally in Paul's mind. He sensed a sudden shifting in gravity, as if the room had been tipped several degrees, and a harsh colorless light filled the room. The light was somehow alive; he felt it sensed his presence, and regarded him as worthless, impure. The light was both a living thing and a process, one he knew with utter certainty must be stopped. He took in the cabinets, saw Mike and Neve motionless on the floor, then Farson was rushing toward Beynon.

The occultist dodged the first swipe of the baseball bat and shot out a leg, tripping Farson. The detective recovered quickly, however, and struck Beynon on the back of one knee, so that he collapsed with a yell of outrage. Mike shot out a hand and grabbed Beynon's ankle, startling the occultist. Farson took advantage of the opening and hit Beynon hard on the side of the head. A sickening crack felled the man instantly, and he lay unmoving as Mike stood up groggily.

"Playing possum," he explained. "Is he dead?"

"Yes," said a small voice. "Now, he's inside the thing he wanted to control."

Ella Cotter emerged from behind one of the metal cabinets, looked down at Beynon. Behind her, the swirl of faces became even more turbulent. For a moment, Palmer's face, huge and pale, appeared. Then it seemed to flow and become Beynon's, the occultist's features distorted with rage and effort. Paul felt sure an epic battle for control of the gestalt entity was taking place. Voices, infinitely distant, wailed in distress, and he tried not to think of what Palmer's company of slaves were suffering.

But whoever wins, it's bad news for us ordinary decent folk.

He and Mike lifted Neve and carried her outside, followed by Ella. Behind them, the white light grew brighter, the swarm of faces hard to make out in the intense glow. Neve stirred, moaned, and Mike helped her sit up. She caught sight of Ella, reached out to her, and the girl bent down to embrace her mother.

"Can we go now, Mummy?" Ella asked. "I'm scared."

"Maybe we've done all we can for now," Farson said uncertainly. "Since there's a child in danger..."

"No."

Neve Cotter's voice was startlingly hard, cold. She was holding Ella at arm's length, staring into the girl's face.

"No," the woman repeated, shaking the girl, who started to whimper. "No, don't try that. You're not my daughter."

"Mummy!" pleaded the girl.

"For God's sake, woman," Farson began, but Paul grabbed his arm, then pointed to Ella's wrist. There was a red welt around it.

"It's not Ella," Paul whispered urgently. He pointed to the vortex. "Ella's in there."

The girl looked up at the three men, gazing from one to the other, then focused on Paul.

"It doesn't matter," she said. "You can't get her back now. They're fighting each other, maiming each other. Whichever one wins will be wounded, weak. Then I can kill them, send all the dead ones away. After that, I'll live out my life, the way I was meant to."

Paul felt a deeper chill than anything the Palmer entity could inflict.

"No," he said. "No, you don't have the right to another's life. And even if you did, it wouldn't be enough. Would it?"

Ella's face was impassive.

"No," Paul went on, "you'll want another life, when you get old, or bored, or that body gets sick. And you'll take one. And another. A psychic parasite, stealing lives down the centuries. As bad as Palmer or Beynon, in your way."

Liz-Ella frowned, tilted her head to one side. A vicious slap from an invisible hand jerked Paul's head to one side. But it did not knock him down. He took a step forward, and she struck him again, sent him staggering back with a blow to the chest. Again, though, he sensed hesitation, and for the first time saw doubt in the childish features.

"You can't kill me, Liz," he said, advancing again. "You know what happens when you kill innocent people?"

"Shut up!" Liz-Ella exclaimed, but this time the mental blow was misdirected, weaker, and Paul barely faltered.

"You go to hell when you commit a sin, don't you?" he persisted. "That's what you were raised to believe—the wicked go to hell."

"SHUT UP!" yelled the girl, putting her hands over her ears.

Mike and Farson exchanged a look, then grabbed her, lifted her off her feet. The girl lost all composure and started kicking and screaming. Glass shattered around Paul. Then a chunk of plaster erupted from the wall. Neve, still sprawled against the wall of the corridor, looked on in despair and confusion.

"Don't worry," Paul said. "I'll bring her back. Come on, guys. I've got a plan."

"We're going in, yeah?" gasped Farson, struggling to keep the girl's feet off the ground. "Then what?"

Paul did not reply. Instead, he reached out and took the girl's hand, despite her efforts to break free. In the brilliant white light, he could see she was terrified. He remembered how young she had been, and how innocent, before Palmer transformed her with his perverted experiments. It was way past time for her to find some lasting peace.

"Okay, guys, let's overload this shitty excuse for a god."

He walked forward into the storm of souls, hand-in-hand with Liz, dragging the girl forward in Ella's body. He felt Farson and Mike let go of her, then desperately battle to keep up, hands raised to protect their faces from the light. There was a clatter as a baseball bat fell onto the tiled floor. Paul flinched as the piercing chill of the entity cut through his winter clothes, dulling sensation in his face and hands.

"Liz," he said, struggling to get out the words. "Do what you should have done when those stupid boys were in danger. Do the right thing."

Then he was truly inside the roiling madness that was the Palmer entity, no longer a dark deity but a battleground of fearsome radiance. He sensed rather than saw the deranged doctor on one side of the struggle, Beynon's icy presence on the other. And trapped between them, their paramental slaves, confused and hurting, damaged beings yearning to break free.

Palmer, the Dark Deity, struggled against the usurper Beynon. The long-dead doctor had experience, resolve, ruthlessness. But Beynon, Paul could sense, had more than a human lifetime's worth of accumulated knowledge. For decades, the book dealer had been refining his occult powers, an area in which Palmer had always been a gifted amateur. They were well-matched, and as they fought, the hapless souls caught between them suffered even more torment as they were torn first one way, and then the other. The nucleus of Palmer's power had already been stripped away by Beynon's initial assault, but the doctor's vast ego was struggling for its very survival.

Despite his best efforts, Paul felt his fingers start to loosen their grip on Ella's hand. He needed to keep Liz inside this purgatory, force her to fight and liberate Ella, and all the lost souls. But now she was gone, and all he could see were fragments of minds drifting around him in a storm of rage and confusion. He reached out, trying to rally the captives to his cause, trying to tell them this might be their only chance to break free, to find some kind of salvation.

He plunged into the tormented thoughts and memories of a dozen or more people. He glimpsed pain, fear, hate, the negative emotions that Palmer targeted and used as leverage over his victims. He almost despaired, searching in vain for some sign of hope. Then, for the briefest of moments, he glimpsed a little girl's face, and a pink umbrella. He reached out to the mind behind the image, sensed a powerful intellect.

Freedom.

It was the one thought, pure and simple, that he could project. It was the one thing that mattered most, to Paul, to Liz, to all the captives of Palmer. He hoped it would spread among the victims while their captor was distracted. With freedom would come disintegration, the end of slavery-in-death to Palmer or Beynon. All Paul had to do was convince the victims to escape, rebel, and thus destroy the foul entity by becoming, albeit briefly, a Deity of Light.

Freedom.

Another prisoner grasped at hope, struggled against Palmer. Around Paul swirled chaos and suffering and turmoil. But he also sensed his friends, those who cared, those who would risk everything for the cause. And there was Liz, her panic and confusion ebbing away as she understood what liberation might mean to her. Palmer and Beynon were still absorbed in their own struggle while he spread the word. He could only pray that neither would grasp the threat to them in time.

Freedom.

***

The cruel white light vanished in an instant, not fading, but ending as if it had never been. Neve Cotter took her fists away from her eyes, waited a few moments in the pitch darkness, fluorescent orange-and-green shapes moving across her field of vision. Then the lights came back on, and she stood up, went back into the room.

The first thing she saw was Brockley Whins, his body crumpled into a sickeningly unnatural shape, half-concealed by a toppled and smashed metal cabinet. Then she saw Beynon, lying like a carved figure on a tomb, arms crossed over his chest, legs together, face expressionless. For a terrible moment, she thought he was going to open his eyes, get up, and take her willpower once again.

Instead, a pungent odor rose from the black-clad body. Beynon began to rot, flesh blackening and falling off the skull and jaw, hair dropping away in clumps. A foul stench filled the room as Beynon's age caught up with him, and the time he had staved off for so long claimed its prize. Covering her mouth and nose, Neve turned away, gagged, tried not to throw up.

"Mummy?"

Ella appeared from behind one of the tall cabinets, her eyes wide, a large purple bruise forming on one side of her face. The girl raised a hand to the discolored skin, flinched, and made a little mewling noise when she touched it. The reaction was familiar, one Neve had seen a hundred times.

"I think I fell onto the computer, Mummy," the girl said plaintively.

Neve said nothing for a while. She had her daughter back. She was aware of others, of Paul and Mike and Farson, gathering round and guiding her gently out of the room. After that, there were more voices, unfamiliar people talking, urgent questions being asked. Then she and Ella were being looked after by two kindly men in uniform, who made them hot, sweet tea and asked them nothing, just put blankets around their shoulders.

"Can we go home?" Ella asked the older of the kind men.

"Course ye can, hinny," the man exclaimed, his Tynecastle accent strong and as sweet to Neve as the tea. "You've done nowt wrong, have ye?"

"No," said Neve firmly. "She's always been a good girl."

***

"The phrase 'Bang goes my pension' seems applicable," said Farson as the police car stopped at a working traffic light. They had already passed two junctions where damp constables stood in the street, waving cars through or halting them in the old-fashioned style.

"You and me both," Mike replied. "Still, I daresay the dean won't be feeling too judgmental about it all."

Paul thought neither man seemed especially worried about their careers. Maybe sensible, grown-up concerns would kick in later. At the moment, he felt sure that—like him—they were trying to readjust to mundane reality after their glimpse of a very different world. Even now the impression was fading.

Did I raise some kind of rebellion against Palmer, after he had beaten Beynon? Did Liz bring them both down? Or was she caught between them and somehow destroyed?

All seemed possible, yet no answer seemed adequate. He might spend the rest of his days waiting for the truth to appear. He felt sure the others were in the same boat. Something had happened. They had survived. That much he knew.

Now, he had a life to live.

EPILOGUE

"It's all kicking off up North," said Laura. "Bloody hell, I hope they're all right."

"Probably in the middle of it," observed Mia. "You got any webcams, stuff like that?"

Laura tried, but found the internet seemed to be down throughout Tynecastle. The outage was massive. They bantered a little about people not being able to go online and rage-tweet about their internet failing—surely the greatest frustration of modern life.

"Hang on," Laura said, "I'm getting something. Webcam near the university, it says. A bit flukey, looks like it's the only one online."

An image appeared on the screen, showing a bleak vista. In the middle distance, a couple of police officers were pushing an abandoned car off the highway. Firefighters were dousing a blaze in a small store. People milled around in clumps, many filming the mess on their phones.

"Christ, it's like a failed revolution or something," breathed Laura. "What happened?"

"We may never know, despite all those buggers filming it. Maybe because of them, in fact," said Mia sourly.

"Hey, what's that?"

Laura pointed at the screen, and Mia saw a black object moving rapidly over the heads of a nearby group of gawkers. It looked like a garbage bag carried by the autumn wind, but then it seemed to hesitate in midair. Suddenly, it grew with startling speed until it filled the screen. It was not quite opaque as Mia could see the store fire and streetlights through it. It seemed to expand, a dark amoeba growing pseudopods, reaching out at them through the screen.

"Jesus Christ!"

Mia flinched, but when she looked back at the screen, the mystery object had vanished. *It probably was a garbage sack,* she reasoned. The screen flickered, and the understated studio lights dimmed still more.

"Hang on a minute, I just need some fresh air."

Mia went outside, onto the fire escape. After a few moments, Laura joined her. They looked out over London, hearing the distant roar of the unsleeping capital. Lights flickered here and there, and a sudden chorus of car horns rose, fell. Then the cityscape was normal again, or at least so far as Mia could tell.

There's something wrong, she thought. *Something has changed.*

But eventually, she gave up gazing out at the vast sea of light, wondering if the pale cloud now looming over the heart of the city heralded more bad weather in the morning. Soon, she forgot her ominous thoughts of the previous night.

***

"No eating ice cream until all hours," said Neve, holding a warning finger in front of Ella's face. "I want you safe in bed by ten."

Ella scrunched up her features.

"Okay, Miss Nearly-A-Teen, ten-thirty at the latest."

"It's not even a school night, Neve," said Mike, picking up his keys from the bowl on the mantel.

"That's not the point, honeybun," Neve said evenly, getting her purse. "It's a question of good sleeping habits."

She looked pointedly at Paul, who was trying to be inconspicuous at his improvised desk by the TV.

"I hope you're taking notes, Mr. Mahan."

Eventually, they left, and Paul continued his online tutoring while Ella watched one of her favorite documentaries. Occasionally, she threw a question over to Paul. He replied that, yes, psychic powers are probably confined to humans and cats. No, dinosaur ghosts probably aren't real, and finally, that he had no idea if Mike was going to propose to Neve, but maybe she would propose to him.

"Because that's allowed nowadays, you know," he added helpfully.

"Sarcasm is the lowest form of wit, that's what Oscar Wilde said," Ella pointed out.

"But the highest form of intelligence, is how the quote ends," Paul shot back. "So there."

They fell silent, and Paul tried to get back to the small and not-too-interesting problems of his online clients. He finished helping one student grasp the fact that the Industrial Revolution had not involved much actual shooting, then wearily moved on to messages. He was about to click on the next in line when he paused, changed his priorities.

'Hi,' he sent to CindyCross008, 'long time no see. You okay? No more nightmares?'

There was no immediate reply, though the site indicated the client was online.

"Away from keyboard," Paul said in a sing-song voice, and moved on. Half an hour later he checked again. A reply had been posted.

'I'm fine. No more nightmares. For now, at least.'

Paul pondered that, wondered if Cindy had had some bad experience during what the media was calling the Palmer Blackout.

'Glad you're okay. How are your studies going?'

Ten seconds ticked away, then twenty.

'I'm learning all the time. Moved to the big city, just finding my way around. Left my previous job, my old boss moved on. Gotta go soon. Things to see, people to do! But thanks for being so kind to a girl who just doesn't seem to fit in. Maybe I'll get in touch again someday.'

Paul smiled, thinking that young people today were intensely fickle and self-absorbed. But then more words flashed up.

'Btw, Liz says hi. We decided to join up when my old boss cashed in his chips. We're having a blast. A bit kinky, I know, but sometimes you gotta go with the flow.'

Paul froze, hands poised above the keyboard. He looked at the generic profile picture of CindyCross008, as if it would confirm his suspicions. As he peered at the tiny square, the image flowed, darkened, and became a black silhouette. Then his laptop shut down.

Paul had spoken to Farson about Beynon's 'Dark Lady'. It had never occurred to him that such a being might impersonate a girl online. But now he had to wonder. Now free of its master, was the mysterious entity, active in the world? And was the Dark Lady 'having a blast' with Liz? Paul struggled to grasp what might be going on elsewhere, happily far away from him and his friends. He was basing an awful lot of supposition on what might simply be an online prank.

And what could I do about it, anyway? I've done my bit for the forces of light.

He thought back to the origins of it all, the desperate desire of a lonely little boy, Miles Rugeley Palmer, to impress a cold, distant father. But was that truly the beginning of it all? Rookwood Asylum had been built on a site sacred to an ancient god whose name was long forgotten. And if the beginning of a story had no neatness, no absolute clarity, why should the ending be any tidier?

Paul stood up, walked over to the sofa, gazed at Ella, unsure of what to say. The girl glanced up, looked back at a herd of elephants forging a muddy river. The voice of David Attenborough described the ways of nature, yet nature remained ancient and mysterious, transcending the mere human.

"You're done for the evening?" she asked.

"Yeah," he said finally. "I'm done. For now, at least. Hey, want to finish off that ice cream?"

* * *

If you enjoyed the book, please leave a review. Your reviews inspire us to continue writing about the world of spooky and untold horrors!

Check out these best-selling books from our talented authors

Ron Ripley (Ghost Stories)
- Berkley Street Series Books 1 – 9
  www.scarestreet.com/berkleyfullseries
- Moving in Series Box Set Books 1 – 6
  www.scarestreet.com/movinginboxfull

A. I. Nasser (Supernatural Suspense)
- Slaughter Series Books 1 – 3 Bonus Edition
  www.scarestreet.com/slaughterseries

David Longhorn (Sci-Fi Horror)
- Nightmare Series: Books 1 – 3
  www.scarestreet.com/nightmarebox
- Nightmare Series: Books 4 – 6
  www.scarestreet.com/nightmare4-6

Sara Clancy (Supernatural Suspense)
- Banshee Series Books 1 – 6
  www.scarestreet.com/banshee1-6

For a complete list of our new releases and best-selling horror books, visit www.scarestreet.com/books

See you in the shadows,
Team Scare Street

Made in the USA
Middletown, DE
03 August 2023

36018853R00097